diSh #2

friends, cooking, eating, talking, life.

 Turning Up the Heat

D0888240

Grosset & Dunlap

Turning Up the Heat

iends, cooking, eating, talking, life.

By Diane Muldrow

Illustrated by Barbara Pollak

For Jean Lemmey—D.M.

Library of Congress Cataloging-in-Publication Data is available.

ISBN 0-448-42816-4   A B C D E F G H I J

Molly and Amanda Moore were hanging 130 feet in the air. Swaying back and forth under the hot sun. Going nowhere on a Ferris wheel that was older than their grandparents.

"*Aaaagh!*" cried Molly. The twins' caged car suddenly dipped, rolled back up, and stopped with a jolt.

"I can't look down," whispered Amanda, Molly's twin. "I feel sick. Stop this thing!"

"It *has* stopped," Molly replied. "You can open your eyes now, Manda!"

Amanda squeezed her eyes shut even tighter.

"Come on, we have a great view of the ocean from up here!" Molly said.

Amanda shook her head.

"Anyway," continued Molly, "you shouldn't have had an entire hero. Or the saltwater taffy after that!"

"I know," Amanda mumbled. "Don't remind me."

Suddenly, the car dipped.

"*Whoa!*" Amanda shouted. Her face turned almost as green as her T-shirt. She grabbed her sister's arm. Hard.

"Ouch!" yelled Molly. "Your *nails!*"

"Sorry," Amanda said, loosening her grip.

The Ferris wheel, or Wonder Wheel as it was called at Coney Island in Brooklyn, New York, stopped again.

"Hey, look!" said Molly. "I see Shawn and Peichi." She waved to their friends down on the ground. "I think they're laughing at us!"

"Now I know why they didn't get on with us. They've been on it before," Amanda said.

Finally, the girls' car made it to the bottom.

"Get me out of here!" cried Amanda as the tattooed ride operator unlocked the car door.

She ran out and took a deep breath of air. She reached in her back pocket for a scrunchie and put her thick brown hair up into a high pony, just like Molly's. Now Molly and Amanda looked more like the identical green-eyed, fair-skinned, freckled twins that they were—identical, that is, except for their clothing styles. Amanda was wearing lime-green beaded bracelets halfway up her arm, white short shorts, and a glimmering green top with a big butterfly on the front. Her beaded flip-flops matched the color of her top and bracelets.

Molly, whose real name was Amelia, loved wearing comfy clothes—like baggy jeans. Lately she was into collecting boys' canvas low-top sneakers in every color she could find: fire-engine red, mustard yellow, pine green. Today she was wearing her favorite faded cutoffs, orange low-tops, an orange sparkle T-shirt that said

"Rock Star" on it, and a blue camouflage bandanna over her dark brown hair.

"Okay. I feel better now," announced Amanda.

"Come on," Molly said, poking her sister. "Tell me you didn't have a *little* fun. I mean, Mom rode this same ride when she was a kid. That's kind of cool, isn't it?"

Both girls smiled as they pictured Mom as a goofy kid in her long braids and funny 1970s striped shorts, the ones she wore in an old camp photo. The girls kept that photo in their bedroom, in a frame on their dresser.

Amanda shrugged and put on her shades. She looked toward the boardwalk. "Where'd Shawn and Peichi go?" she asked. "I don't see Mr. Jordan, either." Mr. Jordan was Shawn's dad.

Molly stood up on her toes and stretched her neck. "I see them. They're talking to someone, but I can't tell who." Molly grabbed her sister's arm, pulling her through a group of rowdy kids and up a ramp to the boardwalk. They found Peichi and Shawn talking to Connor and Omar, two boys they knew from their summer cooking class, and a bored-looking teenager who looked as if he were Omar's brother. Mr. Jordan was a few yards away, in line to buy something to drink.

"Hi!" called Peichi as the twins got closer. "Omar was

just telling us that there's a sideshow around the corner!"

"A *side*show?" Molly asked. "What's that?"

"It's like a theatre, but really wacko! It's called Sideshows by the Seashore," Omar explained.

"Yeah," Peichi said. "They saw this guy, he had tattoos all over, even on his *face*, and he hammered a nail into his tongue!"

"*Oooh*, gross," exclaimed Amanda.

"No way," said Molly, rolling her eyes. "It's a trick!"

"No it isn't!" insisted Omar. He looked at Connor for help. "Tell them, Connor!"

Connor nodded. "He really did it!" he exclaimed. "Go see him! He's called The Human Blockhead. He eats glass, too! And there's other cool stuff. Like a snake charmer who walks around wearing this humongo python."

Shawn shuddered. "Get outta here!" she exclaimed. "Is it alive?"

"Oh, yeah!" replied Connor. "It's the fattest, longest, biggest snake I've ever seen."

"Check it out," suggested Omar. Then he nodded at his big brother, who was beginning to look impatient, and said to the girls, "We gotta go. Later."

"See you in class," said Molly and Amanda. They looked at each other and laughed. They were doing their "twin thing" again. That's what they called saying the same thing at the same time, or reading each other's minds.

"Yeah, later," said Connor. "Let's get something to eat, guys." The boys walked off.

Shawn turned to the girls and giggled. "I hope they don't go home and try eating glass!"

"Let's check out the sideshow!" cried Peichi. She looked around at all the girls. "Do you think your dad would take us, Shawn?"

Shawn giggled. "I doubt it. It doesn't sound like the kind of thing my dad would want me to see! He'd probably make that *face*." She raised one eyebrow and pursed her lips, imitating how Mr. Jordan looked when he didn't approve of something.

The girls laughed. It was hard to picture serious Mr. Jordan at a sideshow, peering through his thick, preppy eyeglasses at a gigantic snake or The Human Blockhead. Then again, he *had* been cool enough to bring them to Coney Island, and take them on the scary old wooden Cyclone roller coaster. He'd insisted that they sit in the last few cars, which was the scariest place to be when it *clackety-clacked* slower and slower up to the highest point, then seemed to plunge straight down the other side. The girls had never heard Mr. Jordan laugh so loudly. Of course, while he was laughing and raising his arms above his head, they were screaming.

Molly dug into the pockets of her cutoffs. "We're out

of money, anyway," she announced, looking at Amanda. "We can't do anything else unless it's free!"

"We can walk on the beach," suggested Mr. Jordan, who came up behind the girls and handed out cold bottles of water. "That's free. Come on, I'll take a picture of you."

"Great!" exclaimed Peichi. "I'm so *hot!* I can't wait to put my feet into the water!" She reached down to take off her sandals.

Holding their shoes, the girls followed Mr. Jordan down the steps from the boardwalk. Their feet sank into the sand.

"*Ouch!* The sand's burning my feet!" cried Shawn. She began to run toward the water, and everyone followed her, dodging sunbathers lying on their towels. Finally, the friends reached the ocean, and they turned around to face Mr. Jordan. They put their arms around each other, shrieking at the feel of the cold water rushing over their feet.

Click! went the camera.

"Work it, girls!" joked Mr. Jordan. He kneeled on the sand and pretended to be a fashion photographer as the friends posed and laughed. *Click! Click!*

I hope Shawn gives us copies of these pictures, thought Molly, *to remember this summer by.*

This was the best summer yet, Molly decided, even though it had started out with her and Amanda being bored and kind of lonely. But so much was going on now.

First, Molly and Amanda had found out about kids' cooking classes being held in their Brooklyn, New York, neighborhood of Park Terrace. They signed up right away. And so did Shawn. They met Peichi at class, although they really didn't *meet* her—they had all been in school together forever, but never really *knew* one another until now. Peichi was lots of fun to have around. *And* she had a pool!

They were all having a great time in class, learning how to make things like homemade pasta and roasted chicken.

Then one day, there was a fire at Justin McElroy's house. The McElroys were new to the neighborhood, and Amanda thought Justin was pretty cute. He was the twins' age and would be going to Windsor Middle School with them in the fall.

With Mrs. Moore's help, the twins, Shawn, and Peichi had cooked a ton of food for the McElroys. It really helped the McElroys, because their kitchen was off-limits while it was being repaired. And *that* led to the girls deciding to form a cooking club! They cooked once a week, on Sunday afternoons. They were also writing a cookbook that was sort of like a diary of everything they were learning to cook, at class and at home.

Plus there were pool parties at Peichi's. Trips to the New Jersey shore to see the twins' grandpa, Poppy. Adventures in cooking class. And the girls were getting to be closer friends, all of them.

"Earth to Molly! Hello-o-o!" called Amanda. Molly had that faraway look in her green eyes again, which drove Amanda crazy. "*Molly!*"

Molly finally heard her name and jumped. She looked at Amanda and her friends. They'd been giggling as they'd watched her daydream. Molly blushed. "Uh, what?" she asked.

"We're gonna get something to eat at Nathan's restaurant," called Shawn, who was already walking ahead with her dad. "Come on! Dad's treating everyone!"

The girls ran along the sand back to the boardwalk, and put on their shoes for the quick walk to Surf Avenue. It was time for one of the best things about Coney Island—the hot dogs!

"I love hot dogs," stated Mr. Jordan, once everyone had filed into Nathan's Famous. "Did you know that the hot dog was invented over 130 years ago? And Nathan's has been here since 1916! That's when they held the first July Fourth hot dog eating contest." He pointed at some old photos on the wall. "See, here's Nathan's way back when...look at all the men wearing suits, and the ladies in their big hats and long dresses and shawls. Can you believe that's what people wore to the beach back then?"

"Mr. Jordan, you know *everything*," Molly said.

"Well, I just think all this stuff is interesting," said Mr. Jordan. He turned to Shawn and smiled. "I'm not embarrassing you, am I, Shawn?"

Shawn smiled shyly and looked down. He could read her mind! "No, Dad."

Mr. Jordan was always embarrassing Shawn somehow. But Shawn loved her dad more than anything. She was proud of him, too. He had written a book. It was a history book about jazz music in New Orleans. Shawn liked reading sections of it from time to time, and looking at the photo of her dad on the book jacket. Like Molly's and Amanda's mom, Mr. Jordan was a college professor. And he could also play the guitar, a cool type of music called the blues.

Since Shawn's mom died a few years ago after a long illness, Shawn and Mr. Jordan had to rely on each other more. It hadn't been easy to adjust to life without her mom, but now she and her dad were closer than before. Sometimes Shawn wished she wasn't an only child. But luckily, Molly and Amanda were almost like sisters to her. That helped a lot.

"Here's our order," said Mr. Jordan. "Quick, let's grab those two tables."

Everyone brought their food to the tables in front of a window. Actually, the tables were more like tall, round counters.

"How come there aren't any seats?" Amanda wanted to know.

Mr. Jordan laughed. "This is fast food—they want you in and out, so the next customer can come in!"

"*Mmmm*, this is great," said Peichi. She licked off some bright yellow mustard from the corner of her mouth. "I've never had a Nathan's hot dog before!"

"*Never?*" asked Mr. Jordan. He dropped his mouth open, pretending to be shocked. "A Brooklyn girl like yourself? Well, young lady, it's about time you did! How about another?"

"Um—okay! That would be great!" replied Peichi. Everyone laughed. No one could ever accuse *her* of being shy.

"Anybody else want anything?" asked Mr. Jordan, looking at each girl. "Shawn? No? What about you, Amanda? You're always game for seconds!"

"That's for sure," Molly said, rolling her eyes.

"I'd better not, Mr. Jordan," replied Amanda. "I've had a lot of stuff here today. But thank you."

"Molly?" asked Mr. Jordan. "How about you?"

Molly smiled. "No thanks, Mr. Jordan," she replied. "I'm stuffed."

"Suit yourself," said Mr. Jordan. "Peichi, I guess it's just you and me!"

As Mr. Jordan walked to the counter, Shawn's dark brown eyes followed him.

"He seems to be, um, more like—himself now," said Molly awkwardly. "The way he used to be."

"What?" asked Shawn, turning back to look at Molly.

Amanda spoke up. "Your dad seems, you know, happier now."

Shawn smiled, a little sadly. "Yeah. I think he's feeling a little better these days." The friends saw tears well up in Shawn's eyes, behind her purple cat glasses. "But you know, he still misses my mom," she quickly added.

"Of course," said Molly. She, Amanda, and Peichi nodded understandingly. "He always will, Shawn. But it's good that he's doing better now."

No one said anything.

Molly cleared her throat. "So, Mom's birthday is the day after tomorrow," she said, changing the subject. "What are we doing for her?"

Amanda shrugged. "I don't know," she said. "Dad hasn't said much about it. She'll probably just want to go out to dinner."

Molly's face lit up. "We should have a surprise party for her!" she said.

"Yeah! You should!" said Peichi. "That's a great idea!"

A surprise party? Amanda was thinking. *But surprise parties are so hard to keep secret. Plus, they're really hard to plan.*

"You could have it in the garden," suggested Shawn. "And you could have—"

"Hot dogs!" interrupted Molly with a giggle. "It could be a cookout."

The three girls looked at Amanda as if to say, *Well? What do you think?*

"Yeah, a cookout," she said slowly. "That's what I was going to say." She didn't want to be the only one who thought it would be too hard to do. Mr. Jordan, who'd returned with the hot dogs, gave her a quick smile. He seemed to understand how she felt.

"You could come to Mom's party, too, Mr. Jordan," said Amanda. Mr. Jordan and Mom had known each other since high school.

"Thank you!" he said. "But I think you two need to check with your dad first and see what he's planning."

Molly giggled. "You know what? He probably forgot about Mom's birthday. Dad's kind of like that."

Amanda smiled. "Yeah, it's true," she said.

"My dad's like that, too!" said Peichi. "My mom has to write everything down for him on a big calendar we keep in the kitchen."

"Well," said Molly, "I think this calls for an

emergency meeting of the fabulous Chef Girls! Manda and I can't do this party without you."

That's for sure, thought Amanda.

"Dad will pay for Mom's party," said Molly. "So we can meet tomorrow for sure. Hey, I know! We can *have* the party tomorrow. That way mom will be *really* surprised!"

Tomorrow! Uh-oh! thought Amanda. *Why am I the only one who thinks this is a big deal? I don't think I want to do this!*

After Nathan's, it was time to cross Surf Avenue and get on the subway. This part of the subway line was elevated, not underground. The girls liked seeing Brooklyn from above for a change. At the foot of the subway stairs, they passed Philip's Candy Store.

"Last chance for frozen chocolate-covered bananas!" called Mr. Jordan, waving at the man behind the counter. "This candy store has been here for over forty years! I used to come here when I was a kid and get the taffy apples." He paused on the stairs. "I can't think of anywhere else in the world where you can take the subway to the ocean," he remarked. "Except Tokyo, Japan. I know you can do that in Japan."

"That's my dad, the walking encyclopedia," Shawn said and she slid her MetroCard through the slot on the turnstile. "Oh! I hear the train!"

"Hurry up!" said Molly.

Everyone hurried up the ramp toward the train. They could hear a conductor announce, "Stand clear of the closing doors." The doors would close any moment!

"Let's not rush, girls, there's always another train," said Mr. Jordan, but Molly and Amanda were sprinting toward the doors.

"Hurry, Amanda!" Molly was saying to Amanda, who was slightly ahead.

"Slow down, girls!" shouted Mr. Jordan, running to keep up.

Shawn and Peichi were sprinting now, too, behind Mr. Jordan. Just then, the doors closed. Molly, Mr. Jordan, Shawn, and Peichi didn't make it on to the train.

Amanda pressed against the doors, but they didn't open.

She couldn't believe it! Molly had made her rush. And she didn't even give her a warning that she wasn't getting on. Her mind was probably on that dumb surprise party!

Amanda saw Mr. Jordan mouth, "Get off at the next stop."

Amanda nodded as her train rolled out of the station, away from all of her friends.

chapter 2

*A*manda leaned her head against the door, tears streaming down her cheeks.

I can't believe I ran onto the train without everyone! she thought. *Why didn't I listen to Mr. Jordan and slow down? Why did I have to listen to Molly?*

Amanda pressed her face against the cool glass window of the subway car. It was thirty seconds until the next stop, but it seemed like forever for Amanda.

The doors opened, and she stepped off the train and looked around. She spotted an empty bench on the platform and sat down.

This elevated train stop overlooked a gigantic cemetery. Everything was completely silent. Now Amanda had to wait for the next train to come, and jump on to join everyone.

Minutes dragged by. Amanda was too scared to even look around much. The station was eerily quiet. She just kept looking in the direction the train would come from. *Hurry up,* she prayed.

Finally, she saw the train. It seemed to be moving slowly, but it finally rumbled in. Amanda stood up.

Hopefully, her friends would be waiting for her in the last car of the train.

Cars flashed by. Finally, hers was coming. There they were! Mr. Jordan and the girls were waving. The train stopped, the door opened, and Mr. Jordan reached out his hand to help her on the train. All the girls were saying, "Are you okay?"

"Oh, Amanda, I'm so sorry!" cried Mr. Jordan. "I feel awful!"

"It's not your fault, Mr. Jordan," said Amanda. "Molly and I never should have run ahead of you like that. I'm sorry." She turned to Molly and said, "Thanks a lot, Molly. You owe Mr. Jordan an apology. And me!" She started crying again.

Molly swallowed hard. "I'm sorry, Manda," she said. She felt helpless. She looked at Mr. Jordan. "I'm sorry, Mr. Jordan."

"Well, everything's okay now!" said Mr. Jordan. "Let's all sit down, okay?"

Amanda sat as far away from Molly as she could.

It was only about a fifteen-minute ride back to Park Terrace. The subway car was full of people who'd spent the warm July Saturday at Coney Island, loaded down with coolers, giant lollipops, stuffed-animal prizes, and toddlers conked out in their strollers. Teenagers with wet hair held hands, babies cried, and groups of boys shouted and laughed.

Amanda, Molly, and Mr. Jordan didn't say much, but everyone else on the train was still having fun.

"This is the party train," observed Peichi. "Oh, here we go!" Suddenly the daylight disappeared as the train plunged underground.

"Here's our stop," announced Shawn. Everyone got out of the train and walked through the cool, dark station and up the stairs to the bright, busy street.

"Thank you, Mr. Jordan," said Amanda.

"Yes, thank you, Mr. Jordan," echoed Molly, wishing that for once that she could remember to be polite before Amanda did.

"You're welcome, girls," said Mr. Jordan. He chuckled. "What an adventure we had! And I'm not talking about the Cyclone!"

"Call me," said Shawn to the twins.

"And me!" said Peichi. "Or instant-message me!"

"We will! Bye!" said the twins, and headed to their house on Taft Street.

"Listen, Amanda," Molly said as the girls walked down the street. "I'm really sorry you got separated from the rest of us, but you shouldn't have run ahead."

Amanda stopped walking. "*Me?* Run ahead? What do you *mean?* You were right behind me, screaming at me to hurry up. You could have warned me that you weren't getting on."

"I guess," Molly said. "Sorry."

"What*ever*," Amanda said. She marched up the stairs of the Moores' brownstone, unlocked the door, and headed inside.

There was a note by the phone on the kitchen counter:

> *Hi, bunnies—did you win any prizes?*
> *Dad and Matthew and I went to the hardware*
> *store. We'll be back soon. Lemonade in fridge.*
> *Love, Mom*
> *P.S. Natasha Ross called at 11:30.*

"Whoa! Natasha called? Us?" exclaimed Molly.

"Oh, she's such a pain," said Amanda, forgetting that she was still angry at her sister. "I wonder what she wants? And what's with the 'bunnies?' Mom hasn't called us that since we were three years old."

"Well, Mom's getting older," joked Molly. "Maybe she forgot we're eleven now!"

Both girls reread Mom's note to make sure it really said the word "Natasha."

Last year, Natasha Ross had become the twins' archenemy—Shawn's, too—after she'd told the school principal that the twins had cheated on an important science test. The lie was whispered from one student to another, and it zipped through the school. Then, when Shawn tried to do damage control and explain to people that Natasha had lied, Natasha spread another rumor that Shawn had cheated, too.

But lately, it was becoming harder and harder to avoid Natasha. She'd shown up on the first day of cooking class, was put in the same small group as Molly, and had made Molly miserable. And as if that hadn't been bad enough, the twins then bumped into her in the small town on the New Jersey shore where their grandpa lived! That time, at least, Natasha had tried to be nice, probably because they had tried being a little nicer to her.

Molly's and Amanda's mom had been telling the girls to forget how mean Natasha had been, forgive her, and just be as nice as possible and include her in things. Mom thought that Natasha had a sad life and needed friends. Molly and Amanda knew Natasha needed friends, all right. She really didn't have any since Monica Aguilar had moved away last year. But why was that *their* problem? Plus, they had already tried inviting Natasha over and she blew them off.

"You don't think we should we call Nastasha back, do you?" asked Amanda.

"Of course we should call her back," replied Molly. "We have to. We can't just—*ignore* her."

"We'll see her in class this week," Amanda reminded

19

Molly. "We could just talk to her then. Oops, there's dried mustard on my shirt." She left the kitchen and went upstairs to change her clothes. *Knowing Amanda, she'll change her entire outfit, not just her shirt,* Molly thought.

Molly put her hands on her hips and stared at the phone. *Should we call or shouldn't we call? I hate not knowing what to do,* she thought. *Just call and get it over with!*

Molly flipped through the phone book, found the number, then quickly dialed it before she could change her mind.

"Hello?" It was Natasha.

"Hi, Natasha, it's Molly...um, how are you?"

"I'm okay. Did you get my message?" asked Natasha.

Well, duh, thought Molly. "Uh-huh," she replied. "What's up?"

"Oh, I thought maybe we could get together. If you want to."

Why do you want to get together now? Molly wanted to ask, but instead she said, "Sure. What do you want to do?"

"Oh, anything," replied Natasha.

That's when Amanda came downstairs wearing a red T-shirt and a blue denim skirt. She heard Molly talking, so she went into the den to pick up the cordless extension, then joined Molly in the kitchen.

"Well, a bunch of us are going to cook tomorrow for my mom's surprise birthday party," Molly was saying. "Do you want to come over and help us?" Amanda's eyes got round as she stared at Molly. She fired Molly a look that said, *What are you doing?*

"That sounds like fun," replied Natasha. "What time?"

"We'll have to call you. It depends on when we can get my mom out of the house for a while. Okay?"

As Amanda listened, she felt helpless. Her face got hot. *Thanks a lot for taking over, Molly*, she thought angrily. *Again!*

"Okay. Talk to you tomorrow," said Natasha. She sounded almost happy. "Bye!"

"Bye." Molly hung up.

"Why did you call her?" asked Amanda sharply. "I don't want to invite her over, Molly. Not that she'd come, anyway. Don't *worry* about her!"

"I'm not *worried* about her," said Molly with a shrug. "Anyway, we've got lots of other things to think about. Like—we're throwing a party tomorrow! We have to get Mom out of the house, decorate, and cook! What are we gonna have besides hot dogs and hamburgers? We have to have a birthday cake, too! Yipes! Tomorrow's gonna come too *fast*. Now I'm stressed out!"

"Well, Molly, you got us into this," stated Amanda. "As usual."

"At least we have the Chef Girls to help us," Molly

went on, as she stared up at the clock. "But first we need to talk to Dad as soon as he gets home, and tell him what we want to do."

"What*ever*," Amanda said. Her arms were folded tightly against her chest, and she looked down at the floor. By now, Amanda thought, she should have been used to Molly's schemes. Molly was always so spur-of-the-moment, always dragging Amanda into something they'd never done before. And when Molly's mind was made up, there was no stopping her. But it wasn't fair!

*B*oy, thought Molly, *she's really mad!*

Molly reached into the cookie jar and handed Amanda a chocolate-chip cookie. "Sorry," she said to Amanda. "Again. First the subway, and now this. But I really think everything's gonna work out...okay? You've gotta trust me. Think how fun it'll be to surprise Mom!"

Amanda sighed and looked up. She didn't want to be mad at Molly anymore—it was too tiring!

"Okay," she said. "I guess I'm stuck with having you as my twin, so we're in this together! Come on, let's figure out what we're going to make tomorrow."

Molly and Amanda grabbed two glasses of lemonade and a few of Mom's cookbooks and headed out to the garden. They really loved it when no one was home and they could have the garden to themselves. The garden was long and narrow, surrounded by a high wooden fence. It had a small patio that was taken up by Dad's gas grill, a colorful flower garden that seemed to take up more room each summer, a thick old tree that was about a hundred years old, some lawn chairs, and a picnic table where the Moores liked to eat on summer evenings.

"'Summer Classics,'" read Molly out loud. "*Hmmm.* Potato salad. We could make that. It doesn't look too hard."

"Great," said Amanda as she turned on the hose. "These poor flowers are about to dry up...hey, what about baked beans? They're good in the summer, too."

"Oh, yeah!" exclaimed Molly. "Mom makes great baked beans. Her recipe must be in one of these books."

"We could make a green salad, too," suggested Amanda. "Or a fruit salad."

"But what about the cake?" fretted Molly. "I don't feel like making a layer cake. It'll probably turn out lopsided."

"Hi, girls!" called Mom from the kitchen window.

"Oh! You're home!" Molly cried. "Uh, hi."

"Hi, Mom," said Amanda calmly as she kicked the cookbooks under a chair. She didn't want Mom to know that they were thinking about cooking. Mom was pretty smart. She'd easily put two and two together since her birthday was coming up.

"What are you reading, Molly? I'm glad to see you with a book."

"Oh, just my summer reading," fibbed Molly.

"How was Coney Island?" asked Mom.

"Great!" replied the twins.

"Did you see my note? About Natasha?"

"Uh-huh," replied Molly. "We might see her, uh, tomorrow."

"Oh! Okay," said Mom. She gave them a big smile.

The twins finally got Dad alone when Mom went upstairs with Matthew to listen to him practice the violin.

"So, Dad, what do you think?" asked Molly.

"Sounds great," replied Dad as he leaned back and opened up the sports section of the *Times*. "When do you want to do it—next weekend?"

"No, tomorrow," said Molly.

Dad dropped the paper and sat up in his chair. "A *party?* Tomorrow? That's impossible, girls! We can't invite people to come to a party tomorrow. It's too short notice."

"Well, it wouldn't be a *party* party," said Molly.

"Just a cookout!" Amanda explained. "For, you know, just the family, but Mr. Jordan would come, too. And Peichi's parents. And maybe the Baders." The Baders lived across the street. Ben Bader was Matthew's age, and the boys were best friends. Mrs. Bader was Matthew's baby-sitter.

Dad thought about it. "Well, if it's just a cookout..."

Dad and Amanda were so much alike, thought Molly

impatiently. So *slow!* Both needed a million years to make decisions about the most ordinary things.

Dad took a deep breath and ran his hand through his graying black hair. His blue eyes twinkled behind his glasses. "So it's tomorrow?"

"Uh-huh," replied the twins.

"Well, we don't have much time," said Dad. "We'll need to figure out what we're making, and go to the store. I don't know how we'll do that without your mom knowing, though. She'll wonder where we're going. And we should decorate the garden a little bit, if we can. So we'll have to figure out how to keep Mom out of the house the whole day tomorrow."

Molly's face clouded. *Uh-oh!* This was going to be even trickier than she'd thought. What if the whole thing turned out to be a disaster?

"What are you giving Mom for her birthday, Dad?" asked Amanda. "A big diamond ring?"

Dad laughed. "Not exactly," he said. "She already has one of those, anyway. A little one, that is."

"Then give her diamond earrings to go with it!" said Amanda eagerly. "I'll help you pick them out, okay?"

"Not this year," chuckled Dad.

"Dad, do you even *know* what you're giving Mom yet?" asked Molly, poking him.

"Maybe I do, and maybe I don't!" replied Dad with a smile.

"That means you *don't!*" teased Amanda.

"Anyway, girls," said Dad, "that's *my* problem. What are you going to make tomorrow? Hot dogs and hamburgers?"

"And potato salad, and baked beans, and a fruit salad or a green salad—or both—and cake. And we'll serve ice cream," said Molly. "Is that enough?"

"I think so," replied Dad. He looked out beyond the girls, like he was looking at something far away. "Plus we'll need tomatoes—and onions—and pickles," Dad went on. "For the hot dogs and hamburgers...let's check the fridge to see what we already have. But the first job is to figure out how to keep Mom from finding out!"

To: qtpie490
    happyface
From: mooretimes2
mooretimes2: wuzzup agent qtpie Shawn? How's the happyface Peichi? Welcome to the Chef Girls' chat room.
happyface: hi! How are u?
qtpie490: hi! What's "the dish?"
mooretimes2: the dish is, once again we are on a mission! Operation Surprise Party. Need your help tomorrow bigtime, chef grrrrlz!

happyface: ok!

qtpie490: I'm there!

mooretimes2: one major thing is gonna happen

qtpie490: huh?

happyface: wha?

mooretimes2: Natasha is coming over 2!!!!!!

qtpie490: :-@

mooretimes2: :-@ is right! talk about a surprise party!

qtpie490: LOL

mooretimes2: she called us

happyface: that's cool

qtpie490: hope she's not mean or weird 2morrow!

mooretimes2: she won't B. She probably won't even show up anyway (sez Amanda!!!)

happyface: how are u gonna surprise your mom?

mooretimes2: Dad sez he's taking her out for brunch, just the 2 of them, then he's sending her shopping with a gift certificate to her favorite store, so he can help us. Come over at 11:15 SHARP, ok? Party is at 4. Shawn, is your dad coming? We need a cake recipe that's not 2 hard! Help!

happyface: Can my parents come, 2?

mooretimes2: Of course!!!! ☺

qtpie490: I have a Texas Sheet Cake recipe. Chocolate! ☺ ☺ Grandma Ruthie makes it every summer, yum. She can e-mail me the recipe 2nite! G-ma's wired, she's on e-mail all the time. I'll bring ingredients.

mooretimes2: OK. whew! ☺ GTG, b-b

happyface: L8R

qtpie490: b-b chef grrrrlz

"Come on, kids, we don't have much time," said Dad sharply. "Matthew! Stop running off, and put back that junk food."

Dad had taken the twins and Matthew to Choice Foods to shop for the party. In a total stroke of luck, Mom had decided to jog around Prospect Park this morning before Dad took her out for her birthday brunch at Kari's Kitchen.

Now they were almost finished shopping.

"Do we have everything?" Molly was checking the list she and Amanda had written up with Dad the night before. Matthew was trying to pop wheelies with the shopping cart.

"Cut it out, Matthew!" Molly said. "I have to concentrate on this list."

Hot dogs
veggie burgers
potato chips
pretzels
soda (Especially root
    beer and cream soda!!)
beans
onions
hamburger meat
tomatoes
potatoes

salad stuff
fruit
eggs
milk
sugar
mustard
ketchup
mayonnaise
buns
paper plates, party hats,
streamers!

"I think we have everything," Molly said as she finished running through the list.

"Dad, this is gonna cost like two million dollars," said Matthew.

"Don't worry about it, sport. Let's get in line," said Dad. "Go. Go." He guided Matthew up the aisle to the checkout. Dad seemed to be in a bad mood, but the twins knew that he was just worried about getting back to the house before Mom did.

"Girls, we probably don't have time to put the groceries away," said Dad as he started the car. "So we'll just throw everything in the den. Okay? Then you can bring it into the kitchen after Mom and I leave. Then you're on your own for a few hours until I get back. Be really careful, okay?"

"Yeah, don't burn the house down!" cracked Matthew.

"Okay, Dad," said Amanda.

"Don't worry, Dad," added Molly, laughing.

"Excellent!" said Dad. "There's a parking spot right in front! Now, everybody grab a grocery bag."

Well, duh, thought Molly. *We're not babies. Dad must be really stressed-out.*

Dad led the way to the front door, put down his grocery bags, and reached in his pockets for his keys. He reached deeper. There was no familiar jangle of keys. "Oh, no," he muttered. He quickly looked left and right, as if hoping to see the keys magically appear.

Amanda felt her hands go cold. Molly felt like a bowling ball was sitting in her stomach. They looked at each other worriedly as Dad reached in his other pocket. Matthew was clueless. He was waving at Ben, who was across the street, and making stupid faces at him.

"Uh, Dad," said Molly. "Don't you have your house keys?"

"They're not here!" moaned Dad. "Where could they be? I thought they were with my car keys." He looked anxiously up the hill to see if Mom was coming. "Great! Now we can't get in until your mom gets home!"

"Well, what are we going to do?" cried Amanda. "The whole surprise will be spoiled!"

Molly looked down at the ground and tried not to giggle, but she couldn't help it. It was just something she did when she got stressed-out.

Amanda wasn't laughing. "Molly! What are you *laughing* for!" she cried.

Dad was still looking around for the keys, checking his pockets for the millionth time.

Molly looked at Matthew.

"I have an idea," she said.

"Oh, great," groaned Amanda. "Just what we need, one of your brilliant ideas."

"No, this will really work!" insisted Molly. "We'll open the bathroom window on the side of the house. Matthew can probably fit though there. And then he can unlock the front door!"

"Cool!" exclaimed Matthew. "I'll break into my own house!"

Dad nodded his head and smiled. "Way to go, Molls," he said. "Let's hurry!"

The family ran around to the side of the house. Dad tried to push up the bathroom window.

"*Unh*," he grunted. "This is—really—stuck."

"Do ya want me to help ya, Dad?" asked Matthew. "I've been doing push-ups with Ben. Look at my muscles!"

No one looked.

Dad kept pushing, and his face turned redder and redder.

"Dad! Take it easy!" cried Amanda.

"*Oof!*" Dad pushed even harder. Finally, the window opened with a loud pop.

"Okay, Matthew, in you go," said Dad, lifting Matthew up. "I'm so glad we never got a new screen for this window." Matthew put his head and shoulders through the opening.

"He fits! All *right!*" cried Molly.

"Hold on to me, Dad!" said Matthew. "Don't let go!"

"Grab on to the heat pipe," said Dad. "I'll push you in slowly. Brace yourself with your foot on the wall."

Matthew got all the way in. "I did it!" he cried.

"Go, Matthew!" cried Dad and the twins. They turned and headed for the front door.

A few seconds later, Matthew opened the front door. They grabbed the bags and ran to stash them in the den.

As soon as they were done, Mom came in, still breathing hard from her run. *Phew!* Just in time!

"Oh, hi, honey!" said Dad. "How was your run?"

"Hi, Mom! Did you run all the way around?"

"Hi, Mom, are you sore?"

"Mom, you don't smell so good."

Finally, Mom and Dad were gone (at least for a few hours!), and Matthew was riding his bike with Ben. Shawn had just arrived with the Texas Sheet Cake recipe and a bag of pecans, and Peichi was on her way.

"Oops!" said Molly, slapping her forehead. "We forgot to call Natasha."

Just than, the doorbell rang. "That's Peichi," said Molly. She ran to the door. But when she opened it, Natasha was standing there, wearing blue cargo shorts and a pink T-shirt.

"Hey!" she said.

"Natasha!" exclaimed Molly. "Hi! I—um—I was just going to call you!"

"I guess I should've waited for you to call, but my mom's been on the phone all morning. So I just thought I'd come over." Natasha tucked her blond hair behind her ears and cleared her throat.

"That's cool. Did you run here?" Molly asked, looking at Natasha's running shoes.

"Sort of," Natasha replied.

"Well, come on in," Molly said. "We're about to start cooking."

"Cool," said Natasha softly as Molly led her down the

long hallway to the kitchen. The radio was blasting and Amanda and Shawn were talking and laughing loudly.

They suddenly stopped laughing when they saw Natasha, not Peichi, walk in.

"Oh, hi, Natasha!" said Shawn.

"Hi, Natasha!" echoed Amanda. "Um, how are you?"

"I'm okay," replied Natasha. "How are you?" She smiled, and for the first time, her light blue eyes didn't seem so cold.

Get outta here! thought Shawn. *Natasha actually looks happy...for once!*

She's actually pretty when she smiles, thought Amanda.

"This kitchen is so nice!" exclaimed Natasha, looking around. "I love it. No wonder you guys like to cook."

'I love it?' thought Molly. *Hold the phone—what have they done with the real Natasha? This can't be her!*

"Yeah, it's great," said Molly proudly. "Our mom decorated it. Amanda and I spend more time in here than we do in our room! We do our homework in here, play games in here..."

"Um, I can see why," said Natasha, as her eyes traveled slowly around the room. She seemed to take in every detail: buttery yellow walls bordered with deep blue and green tiles from Spain. Rugs shaped like apples and pears adding cheerful patches of color to the glossy wooden floor. Funky old dishes and bowls displayed behind cupboards with glass doors. Gleaming copper pots dangling from a large iron rack that hung from the high ceiling.

Suddenly, no one knew what to say next. Someone cleared her throat. Just then, the doorbell rang.

Saved by the bell! thought Molly. "I'll get it!" she said. "That's Peichi."

"Hi, Chef Girls! Hi, Kitty! Here, Kitty, Kitty!" called Peichi, she came down the hallway. Matthew's cat, Kitty, came skidding in ahead of her. She was always trying to get away from Peichi.

"Hi!" said everyone.

"Nice top," noted Amanda.

"Thanks! Hi, Natasha!" said Peichi. She didn't seem at all surprised that Natasha had actually showed up. But that was Peichi. Nothing fazed her. Natasha hadn't been so nice to Peichi at that first cooking class earlier in the summer. But Peichi let it roll off her back. She was the most happy-go-lucky person the girls knew.

Peichi looked at her friends. Her shiny black hair was swept up into a high ponytail that divided into three thick braids. She was wearing a denim skirt, a blue camouflage T-shirt, and hot pink beaded flip-flops. Her dark brown eyes shone. "Are we ready to cook?" she asked. "What are we making? This is gonna be fun!"

"First we should chop the pecans for the cake and get it out of the way," said Shawn. "Peichi, can you help me?"

"Okay. We can practice the knife skills we learned in cooking class," said Peichi. She and Shawn watched each other as they each took a handful of the nuts and carefully took turns chopping.

"This is pretty easy," said Shawn. She finished chopping through her nuts, then chopped through them once more to make smaller pieces.

"Natasha and I could start the baked beans," said Amanda.

"Sniff!" joked Molly. "Does that mean I'll have to peel all these potatoes for the potato salad? Somebody grab a peeler and help me." She pulled open a drawer and brought out two potato peelers.

"I'll help you," offered Natasha, taking one of the peelers. "Then I'll help you, Amanda."

"Oops," said Molly. "I almost forgot, I need to put the water on to boil first."

Matthew and Ben came running into the house. Their feet stomped all the way down the hall to the kitchen.

"Whatcha making?" asked Matthew.

"Yeah, whatcha making?" echoed Ben.

"Chocolate cake, potato salad, and baked beans," replied Amanda, not looking up from her work.

"Beans, beans, they're good for your heart, the more ya eat, the more ya—"

"Oh, you're so funny," interrupted Molly. "Why don't you go annoy someone your own size?"

The girls laughed.

"C'mon Ben, let's go look at your bug collection." Matthew and Ben ran back down the hall and slammed the front door.

"Hey," said Peichi as she cracked an egg into a big green mixing bowl. "Does anyone want to see a movie tonight? Oh, rats! I got a piece of shell in the bowl. I always do that."

"We can't," said Amanda, pouting. "We're broke."

"I know what you mean," said Natasha.

"My parents just raised my allowance," stated Peichi. "*Finally!* But I still never have any money!" Everyone laughed.

"My dad always says, 'When I was your age, my parents gave me only a few dollars to mow the lawn,'" said Shawn, rolling her eyes.

"Yeah," said Molly. "Our dad says stuff like that, too. But then I always say, 'Yeah, but you could get a CD for, like, a quarter back then!'"

"They didn't have CDs way back then, Molly," chuckled Shawn. "They called them albums."

"Or records," added Amanda. "We have all of Mom's in the basement. They're from the 1970s and '80s. Bands had such goofy names back then. Like Bananarama!"

"And Adam Ant!" cried Molly. "Amanda! Let's show them the pogo dance! Our mom really used to do this to music!" She started jumping straight up and down.

Thump! The big bag of potatoes fell off the counter-top and on to the floor. Potatoes went in all directions. Kitty scrambled out of the kitchen with the potatoes rolling after her.

"*Aaaagh!*" cried Molly. "It's the attack of the killer potatoes!" She scrambled to pick them up.

"Settle *down*, Molls," ordered Amanda. "We don't have much time to do everything." She was reading one of Mom's recipes that she'd brought to the store this morning. "Molly, I'm making Mom's vegetarian baked beans recipe."

"But I don't like that recipe," said Molly, wrinkling her nose. "You need to put bacon in baked beans. Or ham."

"I've never had vegetarian baked beans," commented Shawn, as she carefully measured flour, spoonful by spoonful, into a measuring cup.

"Mom made them last summer when our Uncle Roy came over," said Amanda. "He's a vegetarian, and he liked them. *I* liked them. We'll have enough meat at this cook-out, anyway! Okay...first I have to wash the beans." She emptied a package of dried navy beans into a colander and washed them. Then she put them in a large pot and covered them with water.

Molly and Natasha finally finished peeling the red new potatoes. "Good! That's done," said Molly.

"Now what?" asked Natasha. "Do you have a recipe?"

"Mom uses one from this cookbook," replied Molly, taking a heavy cookbook down from a shelf.

"You have a million cookbooks," said Natasha, looking at the shelf.

"Yeah, Mom loves to buy them," said Molly. "She cooks a lot on the weekends. Until lately, that is. She got really busy, and she and my dad started bringing take-out food home, like, every night! So Amanda and I cooked this big gourmet dinner one night. We'd never really cooked before, but somehow we pulled it off without poisoning anyone. And then right after that, we started taking the cooking classes."

"Can I look at a few of these cookbooks?" asked Natasha.

"Sure!" replied Molly. "Meanwhile, I'll find the recipe that Mom always uses." She turned to the index.

Natasha sat down at the kitchen table and began to thumb through a cookbook with lots of photographs. "Look," she said to Molly. "Here's a potato salad recipe that also tells you how to make fresh mayonnaise for it."

Molly leaned over the page. "I wonder if we could make this," she said, scanning the recipe.

"It doesn't look so hard," said Natasha. "Do you have cay—cayenne? What *is* that?"

"I don't know," Molly said. We do have eggs, lemon juice, olive oil...let me check Mom's spice rack to see if we have dried mustard." She opened a cabinet. "Tarragon, pap—paprika...I don't know how to pronounce some of these spices...hey, here's cayenne. I see—it's red pepper. Oh, and we have dry mustard, too. Wow, this looks old." She handed it to Natasha.

"It's probably okay," said Natasha, inspecting the little tin. "Great! We can make our own mayonnaise, if you want to."

Amanda walked over to take a look at the recipe. "It uses raw egg," she said. "Isn't that unsafe?"

Natasha frowned. "Oh, yeah," she said. "Sometimes raw eggs have bacteria in them—"

"Right! That nasty salmonella," exclaimed Molly.

"Maybe we should just use regular mayo from a jar," suggested Natasha. "We don't want people to get sick at your mom's party!"

"Okay," said Molly. "But we could still put the cayenne pepper into the mayo. Now, let's cut the potatoes into small pieces, and then we can cook them...this recipe says to cook them for about fifteen minutes."

"And while the potatoes are cooking, we'll chop the onions and herbs," said Natasha, checking the recipe. "Oops! Amanda, I forgot I was going to help you after I peeled the potatoes."

"That's okay," Amanda assured Natasha as she eyed the recipe. "This is really easy. I just need to cut up the onions." She began to quarter the onions that she would add to the beans.

"Oh, I'm crying," said Amanda. The powerful smell from the raw onion was making tears run down her cheeks. Everyone began to laugh.

"Don't cry, Amanda!" joked Peichi. "Your mom's party is gonna be perfect!" She and Shawn were melting unsweetened cocoa with water, margarine, and shortening.

"Why do we need shortening *and* margarine?" complained Peichi. "This recipe has a *ton* of sugar and fat in it!"

"I know," said Shawn. She giggled. "But I guess that's what makes it so good!"

"Well, anyway, it's not like we eat it every day," said Peichi with a shrug. "Okay, now we have to get a hot pad and pour this melted chocolate over the flour and sugar mixture."

Making the potato salad was easy once the girls had peeled and chopped the potatoes, chopped the onion, and minced the herbs. All Molly and Natasha needed to do after the potatoes were cooked was drain them in a colander, rinse them in cold water, and drain them again. Then they tossed the potatoes with the onion, parsley, and some chopped fresh basil that the girls found in the fridge and decided to throw in. Then it was time to add the mayonnaise. It made the potatoes tangy and creamy. Molly tasted them.

"They need salt and pepper," she said. "That's all." She shook some salt and pepper over the mixture, then took out a clean spoon and handed it to Natasha. "Now you try it," she said. "Do you think it needs anything?"

"*Mmm*," said Natasha. She smiled at Molly. "It's perfect. All we have to do is cover it with plastic wrap and put it in the refrigerator! *Oooh*, I can smell that melted chocolate. Yum!"

"As soon as the cake comes out, I have to put the beans in," said Amanda. She'd drained the beans in a colander and mixed them with mustard and molasses. "What a weird combination," said Amanda. "But it tastes good in the end." She added the onion, canned chopped and peeled tomatoes, and butter. Now the beans were ready to bake! "I hope these beans bake fast," muttered Amanda to herself. "I don't really have three hours."

"Hi, girls!" bellowed Dad over the music. The girls looked up, surprised.

"Hi, Dad!" cried the twins. Amanda lowered the radio.

"Something smells good in here," said Dad. "Actually, lots of things smell good! Is everything going okay?" He set down a heavy bag of ice.

"We're fine, Dad," said Amanda. "How'd it go with Mom? Is she shopping now?"

"So far, so good. We had brunch and then I dropped her off at Leyla's in Brooklyn Heights. I think she'll be there for a while." He smiled and his blue eyes twinkled behind his glasses. "She'll hit the other nice stores around there, too," he added. "Then she'll take the subway home. We won't see her for at least a few hours!"

"Good," said Amanda. "Because we still have to decorate the garden, make the salads, frost the cake—"

"And put a kazillion candles in it!" joked Molly.

Dad smiled again. "I think just a few candles will do," he said. "Your mom will think so, too."

"Oh, *no!*" wailed Amanda a few hours later. "These beans are terrible!"

Mom was due home any minute.

"What's the matter with them?" asked Molly, as she poured a bag of potato chips into a bowl.

"They're hard! And they don't taste like anything," replied Amanda. "What am I gonna do now?" Her stomach tightened.

Dad came rushing into the kitchen. He and Matthew were busy running party supplies out to the garden. Natasha had just gone home without any warning, and Peichi and Shawn were outside helping decorate.

"Where are those pickles? And the ketchup?" asked Dad, his head turning sharply in all directions.

"Dad, my beans didn't turn out," whined Amanda.

"What? Let me see." Dad dipped a spoon into the pot for a taste. As he chewed, he looked away from Amanda and didn't say anything.

"Well?" asked Amanda.

"They're not done yet," Dad told her. "Did you precook these?"

Amanda's face went blank. "Precook? What does that mean?"

"Sweetheart, you have to precook beans. Or soak them overnight. Didn't you do that?"

"No," replied Amanda defensively. "It didn't say I had to do that. See?" She showed Dad the recipe.

"You're right," said Dad, his eyes quickly scanning the recipe. "Well, your mom wrote this recipe for herself. She knows to precook beans, so she didn't bother writing it here."

Tears welled up in Amanda's eyes. "I worked so hard. And now I can't say I made anything for Mom. I hate to cook!"

"You know what?" said Dad, putting his hand on Amanda's shoulder. "We'll keep your beans, and cook them longer tomorrow. And for now, we'll just grab some canned baked beans, doctor 'em up a little bit with dry mustard, brown sugar, and some chili sauce, and they'll taste homemade! Okay? I'm sorry your beans didn't turn out, but you learn from your mistakes, and not just in the kitchen!"

45

"Okay, okay," said Amanda quickly. She wasn't in the mood for a life lecture.

"Looks like we'll be eating baked beans for weeks," cracked Molly.

Amanda fired Molly a dirty look. "I didn't want to have this party anyway!" she snapped. "It's stressing me out! *You're* stressing me out!"

"Hey, hey, calm down," ordered Dad. "Everything's going to work out fine."

"Sorry, Manda," said Molly. "I'm just trying to cheer you up. I'll help you with the new beans."

Amanda exhaled heavily as she watched Dad hurry back out to the garden with a tray full of onions, pickles, ketchup, and mustard. She opened the cupboard door and started moving cans aside, looking for baked beans.

"SURPRISE!" cried everyone later that day as Mom came outside to the garden.

"Oh!" she cried. She began to laugh. "Oh, I can't believe it!" She turned around and messed Dad's hair. "No wonder you told me to go shopping all day," she said. "You *never* tell me to do that!" Everyone laughed.

Mom greeted everyone—Peichi's parents, Mr. and Mrs. Cheng; Mr. Jordan; Matthew's friend Ben and Ben's parents; Shawn; and Peichi—and then gave Molly,

Amanda, and Matthew a hug. "You kids!" she cried,
shaking her head. "You're good at keeping a secret!" Then
her eyes fell on the picnic table heaped with the baked
beans, the potato salad, a fruit salad, a green salad, the
sheet cake...

"Where did all this food come from?"
she asked. She turned to the twins and
their friends. "You didn't make this,
did you girls?"

"Yeah!"

"Uh-huh!"

"We sure did!"

"And Natasha too, but then she left in a hurry."

"And Dad helped out, too."

"Hey! Don't forget about me!" Matthew said.

"Yeah," Amanda said. "Matthew really came *through*
for us today!"

The girls cracked up.

"Well, I—I'm just amazed!" exclaimed Mom as she
looked at each dish. "It smells and looks delicious." She
beamed at the twins and their friends. "I'm so proud of
you girls," she said. "All of you."

"Well, we *are* the Fabulous Chef Girls!" said Molly. "I
can't wait for you to eat everything, Mom! I hope you
didn't eat too much at brunch today!"

"Don't worry, sweetie—all that shopping made me
hungry. Oh, you're the best girls a mom could have."

"*I* can't wait to eat everything!" exclaimed Amanda. She reached for some pretzels. "I hope Dad starts grilling now. You know, we forgot to have lunch."

Dad turned on the stereo and began to put hot dogs, hamburgers, and veggie burgers on the grill, and then it began to feel like a party. As people laughed and talked around them, the twins' eyes met Dad's eyes for a moment. *Whew—we did it!*

The girls went over to the table and helped themselves to the food.

"Matthew, you sure are piling it on," Molly teased.

"Here, put some more paper plates under the one you have," suggested Amanda.

"I can't believe you're not just filling up on hot dogs and hamburgers," commented Molly.

"Well, it's not bad," said Matthew. "You're pretty good cooks." He smiled.

Molly and Amanda looked at each other in surprise. Their freckle-faced little brother wasn't usually one for handing out compliments.

"Oh, *by the way*, Amanda, I saw Justin today," said Matthew as he reached for the potato chips. "Justin, your *boyfriend*. I told him that you're in *love* with him. Ha-ha!"

Amanda turned red. "What?" she said. "Where—where'd you see him?"

Just then, Mrs. Moore appeared and said, "Matthew, I

thought I told you to go upstairs and change your dirty shirt and wash your hands! Go right now, before you eat another thing."

After they had finished eating and cleaning everything up, the girls went upstairs to Molly and Amanda's room to hang out.

"You know, it's so fun to watch people eat all the food that *we made!*" Peichi said. She flopped down on Molly's bed.

Shawn smiled. "I know!" she said. "It's funny that we cooked for all these grown-ups. And they liked it!"

"It was exciting today," said Peichi. "We didn't have much time—"

Mom knocked on the door. "Sorry to barge in," she said. "But I just want to thank you again. Also, I have a proposal for you."

"What's that?" asked Peichi.

"Well, it's an offer. Something for all of you to consider."

"What is it, Mom?" asked Molly.

"How would you like to do what you did today—and get paid for it?"

"Get *paid?*" shrieked the girls.

"Yes, get paid," replied Mrs. Moore. "I need your help.

I have to go on a business trip soon. It's a conference in San Diego, and as long as I'm there, I'd like to stay a few days and visit Aunt Livia."

"Oh, you're so lucky," said Molly. "I miss Aunt Livia. I wish we could go, too."

"I wish you could, too, sweetie," said Mrs. Moore. "But not this time. Anyway, I'll be gone about a week, and I don't want to worry about what you guys are eating—or not eating—while I'm away. Would you like to cook next weekend for our family? Make sure there are enough dinners for about a week? I'll pay each of you and also pay for the food, of course."

"Well," said Molly as she looked at Amanda and her friends. "What do you say? I mean, do we really need to think about this?"

"I'll do it!" exclaimed Peichi. "I mean, I would have cooked for free! But if you want to pay me, I'll do it for money, too!" Everyone laughed.

"We were all just talking about how we wish we had more money," Shawn told Mrs. Moore.

"I don't know, guys," Amanda said. She wrapped her arms around her knees. "Do you think we can handle this?"

"Well, it's a lot of work," Mom explained. "So I think you should get paid for it."

"We can handle it," said Molly and Amanda at the same time. "The twin thing!" they said, laughing.

"Right," said Shawn. "It may take all of next weekend, but we can do it."

"I'll be around next weekend, of course," said Mom. "I'll oversee what you're doing."

"Good," said Molly, relieved.

"What should we make?" asked Amanda.

Mom smiled. "For one thing, I'd like you to bake some cookies," she said. "Matthew won't miss me as much if you make peanut butter cookies— his favorite. And you have the whole week to think about what you'll cook!" She saw the serious looks on the girls' faces. "Don't worry!" she said, chuckling. "I have lots of cookbooks you can look through. And I'll help you think of things to make that aren't too hard. Remember, we did this already for the McElroys."

"*Yes!*" shouted Molly once Mom had left the room.

"I can't believe it," Amanda added. "Not only did the Chef Girls pull off the party, but we just landed ourselves our first gig. *For real!*"

"So the big question is, will Natasha become the newest Chef Girl?" asked Shawn.

"Why not?" asked Peichi.

"Yeah, why not?" echoed Molly as she looked at Amanda.

Amanda nodded slowly and said, "Right. Um, I guess so...she's in...if she wants to be."

chapter 5

The day of their cooking class, Molly and Amanda went to pick up Shawn at her apartment building before they headed over to Park Terrace Cookware, the store where the class was held.

"Go on up," said the doorman, waving them on.

Shawn wasn't ready. She was wearing sweatpants and looked as if she'd been crying.

"What's the matter?" asked Molly and Amanda as soon as Shawn opened the door.

"Come on in," said Shawn, trying to sound normal. "I'm not totally ready yet."

"Is your dad here?" asked Molly.

"No, he just left to go teach. Hang on, I'm going to change." Shawn disappeared into her room.

Molly and Amanda sat down on the sofa and looked at each other. *What should we do?* their eyes said to each other. Shawn didn't seem to want to talk.

A minute later, Shawn came into the living room. She was wearing denim capris and a pink-and-white striped T-shirt. She sat down to lace up her sneakers. No one said anything for a moment. Then Shawn stood up and asked, "Do I look really bad? Are my eyes really puffy?"

"No," said the twins quickly, even though Shawn's eyes *were* a little puffy.

"Come on, Shawn," Molly said. "You can tell us—what's the matter? Is everything okay?"

Shawn rubbed her eyes and sat down again.

"Yeah, Shawn," Amanda added. "You know you can tell us anything."

Shawn nodded. "I know. Thanks. Well, my dad just told me he has to go on a trip. A long one."

"Where?" asked Molly.

"Australia and New Zealand! They're a million miles away."

"For how long?" asked Amanda.

"Like, two months or something. It's for his job. He has to do research for something. I don't even remember what." Her eyes began to tear up again.

"Oh," said the twins. Two months *was* a long time.

"When does he have to leave?" asked Molly.

"Um, not for a few more months, at least. I think Grandma Ruthie's going to come up to stay with me then. But I'm still gonna miss my dad."

"But it'll be fun having your grandma here, right?" Amanda said. "Plus I'm sure your dad will call or e-mail you like everyday!"

Shawn began to cry again. "I know. But that's not the

point. Wh-what if, if—what if something, you know, *happens* to him. He'll be so far away. I just couldn't bear it if..." Shawn sobbed even harder.

Molly and Amanda put their arms around their friend. They didn't know what else to say.

After a while, Shawn cleared her throat, grabbed some tissues, put on her glasses, and said, "Okay, I feel better now. Thanks, guys."

As the friends took the elevator down, Amanda said, "Shawn, if you ever want to talk about anything, you can come to us."

"Thanks, I know," said Shawn with a shy smile. "Now let's go cook!"

Molly, Amanda, and Shawn had to walk quickly to Park Terrace Cookware. They were late.

They got to the door the same time that Natasha did. She was with her mother. Mrs. Ross looked a lot older than the twins' mom. She almost looked like Natasha's grandmother.

I wonder if her mom ever lets her walk down here by herself, thought Molly.

"Hi," said Natasha to the girls. Her mother smiled at them.

"Hi, Natasha," said Molly, Amanda, and Shawn.

"Um, this is my mom," said Natasha. "Mom, these are my friends—Molly, Amanda, Shawn—"

"Hello, girls," said Mrs. Ross. "I'm glad we ran into each other, because I'd like to invite you to our house. For a tea party."

Natasha turned quickly to her mother. She looked surprised. Then she turned bright red.

"Hello, Mrs. Ross," said Shawn. She was the quickest to recover. "I'm Shawn Jordan. I'd love to come to the tea party."

"It sounds like fun," added Amanda. "I'm Amanda Moore."

"Yes," said Molly, remembering not to say, 'Yeah.' "It does. Er, I'm Molly Moore." She cleared her throat nervously, wishing she were as cool around adults as Shawn and Amanda.

"Good!" said Mrs. Ross. "Natasha will phone you about the details later. I don't want to make you late for class."

"Bye," said Natasha suddenly. She turned away quickly from Mrs. Ross and walked through the door. Mrs. Ross's smile faded, and her face suddenly turned hard.

She's mad at Natasha, thought Amanda.

Natasha didn't know about the tea party, thought Shawn. *Now they're mad at one another.*

Yipes, thought Molly.

It was awkward to be standing with Mrs. Ross without Natasha.

"Well," began Mrs. Ross. She looked as if she felt awkward, too.

The twins looked at Shawn with an expression that said, *Help!*

"It was nice to meet you, Mrs. Ross," said Shawn. "Good-bye."

"Bye, Mrs. Ross," said the twins.

"Oh, good-bye, girls. See you soon," said Mrs. Ross, forcing a quick smile as the girls went into the store.

The girls hurried through the large store, which was crammed with cookware, to the back room where the kitchen was. Two rows of long tables, each with wooden tops and long chrome legs, were in the center of the room. Each student had his or her own workstation set up at a table, with a cutting board, butter, one wet dish towel, one dry dish towel, and a container of kosher salt. And in the middle of each table were a few pepper mills and big bottles of greenish-gold olive oil for the students to share.

"That was weird outside," Molly whispered to her sister.

Amanda nodded and then shot a look at Natasha. She stood at her workstation, not looking very happy.

Peichi was already settled in at a workstation. "Hi, Molly!" Peichi said, as Molly picked a station next to her. "I was beginning to wonder if you were gonna show up!"

"Hi," Molly answered. "We just met Natasha's mom outside," she whispered. "She invited us to a *tea party* at their house. You'll probably get invited, too."

Just then Carmen Piccolo, the cooking instructor, walked in. She waved at everyone and put on her chef's apron.

Freddie Gonzalez, Carmen's assistant, came in with her. He seemed to be everywhere at once as he took food out of the refrigerator and measured spices that were stored in clear glass jars in the pantry. He set some pots and pans on one of the kitchen's two large stoves and sharpened some knives.

"Hello, everyone!" said Carmen as she took her place in front of the long tables. As usual, her reddish-blond hair was up in a ponytail.

"Hi, Carmen," said the class.

"Hey, don't I get a hello?" joked Freddie from the stove in the back of the room. "Here are your chef's aprons!" He walked quickly around to each student. "Omar, my man. You ready to rumble, Thomas? Here's your chef's apron, Ms. Peichi! Good golly, Miss Molly!"

Peichi and Molly giggled as they each

took a chef's apron. Freddie was so funny. And cute, too, with his dark brown eyes, short dark hair, and goatee.

Carmen smiled. Her warm brown eyes swept the room, making contact with each student. "Okay!" she said. "We have a special class today. We're going to make an Italian dinner. Is anybody here Italian?"

Several kids raised their hand.

"My great-grandpa moved here from Italy when he was a baby," said a boy named Daniel.

"Where in Italy was he from?" asked Carmen.

Daniel looked up, thinking. "Um, the south," he replied. "A place called Naples."

Carmen nodded. "Naples is a port city in southern Italy," she said.

Molly raised her hand. "We're half-Italian, half-Irish," she said. "Our mom's grandma came here from Italy, from—from—" Her mind went blank. She looked over at Amanda.

Amanda spoke up. "A town called Lucca."

"That's in northern Italy," said Carmen with a smile. "I've been there. It's wonderful there. And guess what— one of the dishes we're making today is from Lucca! It's called 'chicken under a brick.'"

"Chicken under a *brick*?" cried the kids.

"Right!" said Carmen. "But I couldn't find a brick, so..." She held up a couple of big rocks. "we're going to use these!"

"*Rocks?*" exclaimed everyone.

"Then we should call it 'chicken under a rock!'" said Omar.

"You're right, we should call it 'chicken under a rock,'" said Carmen. She laughed. "But that sounds even funnier than 'chicken under a brick!' Don't worry—we're not going to eat the rock. We'll use it to flatten the chicken. We're also going to make a sort of toast called bruschetta, a rice dish called risotto, homemade ravioli—"

"Yesss!" cried Connor from the back row. "I love ravioli!"

"And a salad with tomato, mozzarella, and basil," continued Carmen. "Oh, and biscotti, too! Biscotti are cookies. So let's get started! Count off to three. The 'ones' will do the ravioli, the 'twos' will do the chicken, the 'threes' will do the risotto." Carmen always broke the class into small groups. Each group made at least one dish. And Carmen would often stop class to let everyone watch what one group was working on.

After everyone counted off, Peichi and Amanda were in the chicken and biscotti group, Shawn was in the ravioli and bruschetta group, and Natasha and Molly were in the risotto and salad group.

"Ow! Don't hit me with that rock!" Some of the boys in the chicken group were horsing around, pretending to pound each other with the rock.

"Watch it," Freddie called over to them. "Put the rock down, Connor. No one touches the rock except for Carmen or me."

Peichi and Amanda were the only girls in the chicken group.

"I feel like we're with a bunch of five-year-olds," whispered Peichi.

"Maybe they'll get too rowdy and Carmen will make people switch groups, to break them up," said Amanda. That had happened before.

Meanwhile, in the risotto group, Natasha chopped basil that would go into the dish. Molly began to mince an onion. She still wasn't very good at using a knife. Carmen taught knife skills in class, and every student got a chance to practice. There were always lots of items to cut, chop, and dice.

Carmen stood and watched Natasha and Molly use their knives.

"Pretty good, Natasha," said Carmen. "Molly, just remember that you don't have to grip your knife so hard."

Carmen left to watch the ravioli group.

In a low voice, Natasha said to Molly, "So, now you've met my mom." She didn't look up from her cutting board.

Molly didn't know what to say. *What's Natasha getting at?* she wondered.

Molly swallowed and said, "Uh-huh!...So, you're going to have a tea party."

"Well, I didn't know I was," said Natasha sharply. The other kids in the group looked over at Natasha, surprised.

Weirdness alert! thought Molly. *I knew something strange was going on outside with Natasha and her mom!*

Everyone went back to their work, and Natasha lowered her voice again. "This tea party is my mom's idea. She's so old-fashioned." Then, as if talking to herself, Natasha muttered, "Why can't I have my friends over just to hang out? Everything's such a big deal with her."

"Well, it'll be fun, anyway," Molly assured her. "I've never been to a real tea party. Who else is coming besides the Chef Girls?"

"Maybe you should ask my mom," said Natasha, rolling her eyes. "She's doing this because she—she wants to—check you out! Make sure you're all okay for me to hang out with. It's so embarrassing." She tried to laugh.

Whoa! thought Molly. *We'll be on display. Bizarre!*

As weirded-out as Molly was, she tried to make Natasha feel better. "Don't worry," joked Molly. "We'll all try to act normal in front of your mom."

A smile flickered over Natasha's face.

"Okay, class! Stop what you're doing for a moment," called Carmen, standing near Shawn. "I want to talk to you about the ravioli."

Peichi's hand went up. "What are you going to put in it?" she asked.

Carmen smiled. "I was just going to tell you," she said. "We're going to use spinach for the filling."

"Spinach?" muttered some of the kids.

"Ravioli often has meat in it, but not always," Carmen went on. "And I know you're going to like this. We're going to make the dough by hand today, but you can also make it in a food processor. Shawn has put the flour and salt in a bowl, and Connor has poured in olive oil and some hot water. Now I'm going to shape it into a ball... can everyone see?...and knead it like this."

Carmen quickly kneaded the ball of dough for a few seconds, then said, "Now you try it, Shawn."

"You go, Shawn!" cracked Omar from across the room.

Shawn rolled her eyes, embarrassed. The whole class was watching her. She pressed down on the dough with both hands and worked with it as Carmen had done, but it just felt like it was all ending up on her hands. "It's kind of sticky," said Shawn, looking up at Carmen.

"Okay, we'll do this...there, is that better?" asked Carmen, sprinkling some flour over the dough with her fingers.

Everyone in Shawn's group practiced kneading the dough. After just a few minutes, the dough was smooth.

"Great!" said Carmen. "Now, who would like to practice rolling out the dough with a rolling pin? You, Omar...come over here."

All the boys in the class began to laugh when they thought of Omar using a rolling pin.

"Me?" asked Omar. "No way, man. I'm not in the ravioli group." He was turning red.

"Go ahead, Grandma!" cracked a kid named Ryan. Everyone began to laugh. Even Carmen and Freddie smiled.

"Yo! I'll roll it over your head, Ryan," joked Omar. "All right! I'm gonna do it! Here I come! I'm gonna use a rolling pin!" He strolled over to the table as the entire class began to clap.

"Just do it like this," said Carmen. She rolled the pin over the dough a few times. "Now you try."

Omar clowned as Carmen handed him the rolling pin. He flexed his muscles, cleared his throat, and finally began to roll out the dough. "Hey, this is easy!" he said. "Look. It's getting thinner!"

"Can I try?" asked Peichi.

Omar looked up at Peichi. "I don't know if you can handle it," he kidded her. "You have to be really strong, like me."

"I *am* really strong!" retorted Peichi.

"Come on over, Peichi," said Carmen.

Peichi tried, then handed the rolling pin to Shawn. Soon everyone wanted to use the rolling pin, even the other boys.

"Okay, everyone, the dough is ready now," announced Carmen after a while. "It's as thin as we can get it. Now we'll make the filling. You can go back to what you were doing, and when we're ready to make the ravioli, everyone will get to make some."

It was easy to make the spinach filling. Shawn's group quickly cooked the spinach in boiling water, then chopped it. They heated some olive oil in a pan and threw in some minced garlic. After it had softened, they added the spinach, salt, and pepper. They let the mixture cool, then added an egg, Parmesan cheese, and even a little nutmeg, which was a spice that Shawn had used in cookies before.

"It seems weird to put nutmeg in with spinach and garlic and cheese," she commented to Carmen.

"Don't worry! It'll be good," Carmen assured her. "It just adds a little special something."

Soon it was time to make the ravioli. Carmen stopped the class again so everyone could watch.

"This is the fun part!" she announced.

As everyone hung around the table to watch, Carmen quickly cut the thin pasta dough into wide strips. "Now we'll add the filling," she said. Shawn's group dropped spoonfuls of the spinach mixture evenly in rows on top of half the dough, about an inch apart.

"Don't put too much filling in," warned Carmen, "because when you cook the ravioli, the thin dough can break apart."

Then Carmen folded half the dough over the half with the filling, sealed the sides with her finger, and pressed down to seal the dough between the little mounds of spinach.

"Now we just have to cut it into pieces," said Carmen, brushing some flour off of her hands. She looked up. "Here, Freddie, you do it."

Freddie flashed a smile. "I love this part!" he said, walking toward the table.

He took a pastry wheel, which was just a handle with a wheel at the end that had points all around it. He rolled the pastry wheel through the dough in between the spinach mounds.

"Ta-da!" said Freddie. "Ravioli!"

"The little raviolis look so cute!" observed Peichi.

The boys snickered.

"Aw, so cute!" said some boy, imitating Peichi.

Peichi rolled her eyes.

"Now someone else can try," Freddie said.

"Oooh! Let me, let me!" cried some of the kids, pushing toward the table.

"Everyone can take a turn," said Freddie, handing the pastry wheel to Amanda. "We made a lot of ravioli."

"What are we going to put on top of it?" asked Amanda as she carefully rolled the pastry wheel through the dough. "A tomato sauce?"

"A tomato sauce is a great topping," said Carmen.

65

"Or a meat sauce," added Freddie.

"But today we're going to top it with butter, a fresh herb called sage, and some Parmesan cheese," Carmen went on. "It's so simple, and it tastes great."

"So, why do we put the chicken under a brick? Or a rock? Or whatever?" Peichi had asked Freddie when he'd come by her group's table at the beginning of class.

"It makes a crispy chicken," replied Freddie as he opened a package containing a whole chicken. "We're going to butterfly, or split, this chicken, and marinate it. 'Marinate' means to soak it in a type of sauce to give it flavor."

"What's in the sauce?" asked Thomas.

"Actually, we call the sauce 'marinade,'" said Freddie. "This marinade has salt, garlic, olive oil, and fresh rosemary. Believe me, there's nothing better than rosemary on chicken! Amanda, you can start to make the marinade. Chop this garlic—not too small, please. And Peichi, you can mince this fresh rosemary—"

"*Mmmm!* This rosemary smells so good!" interrupted Peichi, as she held the leaves near her nose.

"Connor," continued Freddie, "I'll help you cut off the excess fat. Then you can wash the chicken and pat it dry with some paper towels. I'll show you how to take the backbone out of the chicken."

"Cool!" said the boys.

"Gross," said Amanda.

"Don't do this without an adult," said Freddie, reaching for a heavy knife. "You can always ask the butcher at the supermarket to do it for you. The breast needs to be face-up...I'll just cut along one side of the backbone from front to back, and take it out...now see how the chicken lays flat?"

Peichi and Amanda combined the rosemary leaves, garlic, and some salt with olive oil, then rubbed the mixture all over the chicken.

"We can put some marinade under the skin, too," suggested Freddie. "Thomas, take a spoonful and slide it under the skin."

"Okay," said Thomas. "That'll make the flavor really come out, right?"

"Right."

"Now what?" asked Amanda.

"We'll refrigerate it," replied Freddie. "Until we're ready to cook it. Now we can start on the biscotti. Biscotti are twice-baked cookies, so they take a while to do. But first you better wash your hands. And don't forget to use soap!"

"I know what biscotti are," Connor as he dried his hands. "They look really hard to make."

"You guys can handle it!" said Freddie. "Here's the

recipe. Just follow it and you'll be all right. Now I'm going to check on the salad group."

Meanwhile, Molly and Natasha's group was busy making the salad and stirring the risotto.

"We're going swimming later at Peichi's," Molly told Natasha. "Do you want to come, too?"

Natasha didn't look up from the risotto she was stirring. "I can't go anywhere," she said. "Except here. I'm grounded for a week. I can't go anywhere except for this class."

"Grounded! Why?"

"Well, I went over to your house without telling my mom where I was going. I sneaked out."

"So that's why you—you left so suddenly yesterday."

"Uh-huh. I started getting a stomachache, 'cause I knew my mom was looking for me and freaking out, so I had to go. I didn't want to tell everyone that, though. Anyway, I got into a lot of trouble when I got home."

"So why is your mom giving you a tea party? I mean, that doesn't sound like a punishment," commented Molly.

Natasha just shrugged, so Molly decided not to ask her any more questions.

Half an hour later, the class was psyched. It was almost time to eat! The risotto was almost ready, the salad was done, the cookies were baking, and the ravioli was boiling. Everything smelled great.

"We're *hungry*," shouted the boys in the chicken

group. They were carefully watching the bread for the bruschetta that they were toasting under the broiler.

"Heads up, everybody!" called Carmen across the room. "We're going to cook the chicken now!" She looked at the bruschetta boys. "Take that out now," she said. "Rub some garlic in, brush the olive oil over the bread, and put a little salt and pepper on top."

Carmen heated some olive oil in a pan. "Here we go!" she said. She placed the chicken in the pan, skin side down, and threw in some garlic and rosemary. "Now we weigh the chicken down." She put a skillet on top of the chicken.

"Now," she said, "my helpful assistant, Peichi, will hand me the rocks."

Peichi giggled and reached for the rocks.

"One rock. Two rocks. Thank you." Carmen set the rocks on top of the skillet that was on top of the chicken. "There! Chicken under a brick! Or rocks, that is. I'm cooking it on a high heat for ten minutes, and then I'll roast it in the oven for about fifteen minutes. All we have to do after that is take the weights off, turn the chicken over, and roast it another ten minutes."

Finally, it was time to eat.

"Who's the hungriest person here?" Freddie asked the class.

"Me!" called Connor.

"No, me!" said Omar.

"Then you guys get to help me take the food out to the table," said Freddie. "You too, Natasha."

So Natasha and the boys helped Freddie put the food on pretty platters and in bowls, and carry it out to the back room. The room was small, and a big table took up most of it. Carmen had set the table with a dark blue tablecloth, blue-and-white china plates, fancy glasses, and cloth napkins that matched the tablecloth.

"Waiter, I need some service," cracked Ryan to Omar as he put the bowl of risotto on the table.

"It feels like Thanksgiving!" said Peichi, giggling. "Natasha! Sit here!" She patted the empty chair next to her.

The first time the class had sat down together to eat, it felt a little funny. Everything looked so fancy and not all the kids knew each other, since they came from all over Brooklyn. But now things were starting to feel less awkward. It didn't seem as strange to eat, talk, and laugh together.

"Yo, man, put your napkin on your lap," Omar told Connor. "And please pass the ravioli!"

"I will, man, chill out," said Connor. Omar and Connor were always kidding around.

Natasha spoke up. "Please pass the 'chicken under a brick'!"

Everyone laughed, and Natasha smiled her first *real* smile all day.

chapter 6

After class, Amanda, Molly, Shawn, and Peichi hung out with Natasha on the sidewalk outside Park Terrace Cookware.

"I'm stuffed," said Molly. "That was great. Especially that ravioli."

"Uh-huh," said Natasha. Her smile was gone.

"Here comes your mom, Natasha," said Shawn.

Natasha didn't turn around. "Can you believe she won't even let me walk here by myself?" she asked. "She thinks I'm five years old."

"Well, I wish you could come over today," said Peichi. "You'd love my pool! And we've made up all these games to play in it. And we're making a video. My dad lets me use his video camera, as long as I'm careful with it—"

"Okay, bye, Natasha," interrupted Molly. She didn't want to talk to Mrs. Ross again. "Let us know about the tea party."

The friends turned around and walked toward Peichi's house.

"So, when is this tea party?" asked Peichi. She was annoyed at Molly for cutting her off. She'd wanted to meet Mrs. Ross and see if she would be invited, too.

"We don't know," replied Shawn. "I wonder if she'll have fancy china? And little cakes?"

"Knowing me, I'll break a teacup," moaned Molly. Everyone giggled.

"What'll I wear?" Amanda muttered.

"Yeah, what do you wear to a tea party?" asked Shawn.

"Don't ask me," replied Molly with a shrug. "I think this is gonna be crazy! Like something out of the tea party in *Alice in Wonderland!*"

"Yeah, Mrs. Ross will be the mean queen," joked Peichi. Everyone cracked up, except Amanda. She was picturing herself walking in Natasha's front door. Mrs. Ross would be standing there with her hands on her hips, staring at her, trying to make her nervous, but Amanda would be looking so cool in her flower-print tank dress...no, her butter-yellow capris with the embroidery along the hem, and white peasant top...

"Manda, are you in there?" Molly was asking. "Hey I'm supposed to be the daydreamer, not you!" Everyone giggled, which startled Amanda out of her thoughts.

"What?" she asked, looking around.

"She's stuck in a fashion fantasy!" cried Shawn.

Even Amanda had to laugh at that one.

"Look!" said Mr. Jordan. "It's a red-tailed hawk!"

"Cool!" said Shawn. "I've never seen one before!"

Shawn and her dad were in Brooklyn's Prospect Park, peering through binoculars at the large, rare birds perched in a tree. Though the day had been hot, the air was cool now. They were having a picnic dinner, just the two of them. Shawn and her dad went to the park all the time, especially in the summer. All around them, parents watched their toddlers run across the grass, teens threw Frisbees, and people of all shapes and sizes showed off their dogs of all shapes and sizes.

"So how was your cooking class today?" asked Mr. Jordan. He and Shawn were eating submarine sandwiches from Pete's Deli.

"It was awesome!" replied Shawn. She told her dad all about "chicken under a brick."

"Ha-ha! That's great!" cried Mr. Jordan.

"We need to start cooking soon for Mrs. Moore," said Shawn. "Did I tell you that she's paying us to cook a bunch of meals for the Moores, 'cause she'll be out of town for a while?"

"Yes, you told me," Mr. Jordan said with a smile. "That's a great idea. You just formed a cooking club, and it's turning into a catering business!"

"A *business*," Shawn repeated slowly. "Yeah, I guess it is."

"What are you going to make?" asked Mr. Jordan.

"Oh, lots of stuff that you can just reheat, or grill. And peanut butter cookies for Matthew."

Mr. Jordan changed the subject. "What do you think of me being so far away in a few months?" he asked.

Shawn took a deep breath. "We-e-ll," began Shawn. She didn't want to start crying again. She knew her dad really didn't want to go away, and her crying would just make it harder.

"I'm not thrilled about it," admitted Shawn. "But maybe the time will go fast. I'll be in middle school then, and—whoa! I'll be in middle school! I haven't even thought about *that* yet!"

Mr. Jordan put down his sandwich. "Shawn," he said, "we've been through a tough time. And if you don't want me to go, I won't. Maybe it is too soon for me to be traveling so far."

Shawn looked down at her potato salad. She felt tears welling up in her eyes. *So much for not crying,* she thought.

"It's okay, honey," her dad said putting his arm around her.

If she said, "Don't go, Dad," would that be wrong?

"You think about it, sweetie," said Mr. Jordan, smiling at her. "I don't even know when I'm leaving. And there's a chance I might not go at all. We've got some time on this."

Shawn closed her eyes and breathed in the fresh evening air. *Everything will be all right,* she said to herself. *Won't it?*

chapter 7

"Amanda, you can't change your outfit any more," Molly complained. "We're gonna be late!"

"*Ohhhhh!*" Amanda ran from the mirror to her stack of magazines. She grabbed one and began to flip the pages frantically. "I can't find anything in my magazines about what to wear to a tea party!"

"That's because nobody goes to tea parties," commented Molly. "Girls haven't done that in, like, a hundred years."

"That's not true. Ashley Harris had one for her birthday last year," Amanda pointed out.

"I don't remember that," Molly said.

"That's because we weren't invited," explained Amanda with a giggle. "Remember?"

"Anyway, you look fine," said Molly.

Amanda ran back to the mirror. It was a fancy full-size mirror that she'd gotten for Christmas last year. Before the twins had gotten the mirror, they'd always had to stand on Molly's bed to see their reflections in the mirror on the bureau. Molly hadn't minded doing that. But Amanda asked for a mirror for Christmas. Now she could easily check herself out whenever she wanted!

"I *guess* I look okay," muttered Amanda, staring at her reflection. She was wearing a pink cotton skirt, a white peasant top with pink embroidery, and white sandals. "But what about my hair? Should I wear it up? It doesn't look right today. *Aaaarrrgh!*"

Molly sighed. She'd tried on only one outfit. It was the rose-colored tank dress with big flowers that she had bought with a gift certificate to the Gap. She'd thrown on some sandals and pulled her hair back into her usual high ponytail. Done.

That's when Mom came in.

"What happened in here?" she asked, looking around the room. Dresses and skirts were piled on the beds. Shoes dotted the rug. "It looks like Filene's department store after a big sale."

"Don't worry, Mom, I'll clean it up when we get home," promised Amanda. "Should I take a pocketbook? Which one should I take? Are you taking one, Molly?"

Molly shook her head.

"You really should, Molly," said Mom. She looked closely at Molly, as if she was inspecting something.

"What?" asked Molly, shrinking back.

"Let me curl your hair, honey," said Mom. "Where's your curling iron, Amanda? Here it is...this'll just take a second."

"I never curl my hair," whined Molly.

"You can keep your ponytail. I'm just curling the end,

okay? It'll look so cute." Mom plugged the curling iron into the wall.

"How do I look, Mom?" asked Amanda anxiously.

"You look perfect! Don't worry!" Mom assured her.

"This tea party is gonna be weird," said Molly.

"You don't know that, Molly," Mom reminded her as she made one big curl of Molly's ponytail. "I think it sounds like fun. And I'm sure that Mrs. Ross isn't the meanie you think she is. Just go and have a good time!"

"Okay!" said Amanda. "I'm ready!"

"Perfect!" said Mom. "Now let's just put a bow in Molly's hair—"

"No way!" cried Molly. "No bows, Mom. We have to go!"

Mrs. Moore smiled. "I miss when you girls wore bows in your hair. Bye! Have fun!"

The twins still had to pick up Shawn. Mr. Jordan greeted them at the door.

"Hi, Molly! Hi, Amanda! You look great! Come on in. I'm going to take a picture of you three when Shawn's ready."

"She's not *ready?*" shrieked the twins.

Mr. Jordan had to laugh, and so did Molly and Amanda. Mr. Jordan shielded his face with his hands and said, "No! Not 'the twin thing' again!"

 77

"Let's go in her room," suggested Molly.

"Here I am, here I am!" said Shawn, rushing into the living room. "Hi guys!"

Shawn looked ready for a tea party with the Queen of England. She wore a black straw hat with a wide brim, a red-and-white polka-dot sundress, and her black wedge sandals.

"Cool hat!" shouted the twins.

Shawn struck a movie-star pose. "Thanks!" she said. "Dad and I were shopping the other day, and we found this store that sells cool old clothes. So I bought this hat and this dress! Okay, I'm ready to go."

"Just a second," said Mr. Jordan. He quickly snapped a photo of the girls. "Have fun!"

"I'd never think to wear a cool outfit like yours, Shawn," Molly told Shawn as the friends rode down in the elevator.

"You look like you're about twenty-five years old, or a famous actress!" said Amanda. She wished she'd thought to do something fun like Shawn had.

"Thanks," said Shawn. "It was really Dad's idea. Well, here we go. I wish Peichi had been invited."

"So do we," said Amanda. "Peichi's kind of bummed out. But Natasha's mom didn't know about her."

"She'll get over it," said Shawn. "Besides, I've never really seen her angry. She's always so *happy!*"

"But I wonder why Natasha didn't tell her mom to invite Peichi?" Molly asked.

"I think it's because Natasha didn't even want the tea party," suggested Amanda. "I don't think it was anything against Peichi at all." She changed the subject. "I wonder what they'll have to eat."

"I'm too nervous to eat," said Molly.

It didn't take long to walk to Natasha's house on Garden Street.

"You ring the bell," said Amanda, poking Molly.

"No, *you* ring it," retorted Molly.

Amanda gave Shawn an extra-sweet smile. "Shawn, would you ring the bell?"

Shawn shrugged. "Why should I be nervous?" she asked. "It's a party! It's not a big deal!"

Shawn led the twins up the stone steps of Natasha's townhouse and rang the bell. Everything seemed so quiet. They listened for footsteps coming toward the door.

"It *is* today, right?" asked Molly anxiously.

"Of course it is," replied Shawn.

Just then, Natasha opened the door and smiled at the girls. Her blonde hair looked so different, because she'd curled it in ringlets. It looked old-fashioned but kind of cool and modern at the same time. For a moment, Molly was surprised. All along, she'd been expecting Mrs. Ross to come to the door, which she'd been dreading.

"Hi!" cried the girls.

"I love your hair, Natasha," said Amanda.

"Hi!" said Natasha. "You all look really nice. Well, come on in."

Natasha, who was wearing a long tank dress like Molly's, only dark blue, led the girls into the house. It was very formal, with thick Oriental rugs, old, polished furniture, large bouquets of deep red and pale yellow roses, and portraits on the walls. The house was really, really neat. It almost looked as if no one actually lived there.

"We're going to be in the garden," said Natasha.

She seems kind of serious, not like someone who's excited about giving a party, thought Amanda.

"Can't we see your room?" blurted Amanda.

Just then, Mrs. Ross seemed to appear out of nowhere. She seemed even taller than before, but her blue eyes were cold.

"Hello, girls," said Mrs. Ross with a little smile. She was wearing a simple pink cotton dress. Simple, but expensive-looking.

"Hello, Mrs. Ross," the girls answered.

"You all look very nice," said Mrs. Ross. "Well, let's go into the garden."

"They want to see my room—" began Natasha.

"Later, dear."

The twins looked at each other as they followed Mrs. Ross. As she walked, she left a trail of rose-scented perfume.

Can you believe this? asked Amanda with her eyes.

No way! Molly's eyes shot back.

In the garden, a man sat reading the paper in one of the wicker chairs.

"Girls, this is Mr. Ross, Natasha's father," said Mrs. Ross.

A man with graying hair stood up. "Hello, girls," he said. His smile seemed genuine, and he seemed much friendlier than Mrs. Ross. "Please sit down," he said, gesturing at the empty wicker chairs.

Molly sat up as straight as she could. She could hear Mom saying, "Don't slouch."

Amanda sat up straight, too. Her hands and feet felt too big. But when she spied the little round cakes with pink icing on a silver tray, she felt better.

Suddenly, Molly wanted to be in a pair of cutoffs riding her bike, in a bathing suit jumping into Peichi's pool, in her pajamas playing Scrabble with Amanda... doing anything but minding her manners, wondering what to say, wearing this dress.

"Where's your dog, Natasha?" asked Amanda.

"Oh, he's inside. I'll bring him out in a bit," replied Natasha.

How weird that the dog didn't run to the door with

Natasha, thought Molly. *Dogs always greet people at the door.*

Silence.

Mr. Ross cleared his throat. "So, Natasha tells us that you have a cooking club. That sounds like a lot of fun." He looked at each of the girls, then his eyes settled on Shawn.

"Yes," said Shawn. She didn't seem nervous at all. "We try to cook once a week, and we're writing a cookbook of all the things we make."

Just then, Mrs. Ross came out holding a big tray with a pitcher of iced tea, a pitcher of lemonade, and cookies. Natasha's terrier came out with her.

"Oh, he's so cute!" exclaimed Amanda. "Come here, doggie! What's his name?" she asked, looking up at Natasha.

"That's Willy!" said Natasha. "No jumping, Willy."

Mrs. Ross began to pour glasses of tea and lemonade and serve the cookies and cakes on little china plates. "Here you go," she said, offering Molly a glass. "Tell us about yourselves...what do your parents do?"

"Um," said Molly. She hadn't expected to be asked what her parents did for a living. "Our mom is a college professor."

"Of what, dear?" asked Mrs. Ross.

"Of—art history. At Brooklyn College. Our dad, he, um, works with computers and stuff, I mean, things."

Molly's toes curled. "I'm not really sure what he does, exactly—"

"He designs websites and helps fix people's computers," Amanda broke in. "He works for an architecture firm."

Thank you! said Molly with her eyes.

"How interesting," said Mrs. Ross. She turned her gaze to Shawn. "And your parents, dear?"

"My father is a professor at Brooklyn College, too," said Shawn. "He teaches about ancient peoples. He's called a—a cultural anthropologist." She hoped Mrs. Ross wouldn't ask about her mother. Luckily, Mrs. Ross left it at that.

"Well," she said to the girls, "your parents all have such interesting jobs. Mr. Ross is an attorney for Whitney, Deardorf, Ross, Cox and Finkelstein. He's a partner, of course."

Natasha rolled her eyes.

A partner to what? wondered Amanda, as she nodded her head.

Ask me if I care, thought Molly, as she smiled politely.

Shawn smiled. "Oh, that's nice," she said, as if Mr. Ross' job was the most fascinating thing she'd ever heard of.

No one said anything for a moment.

And no one noticed the squirrel that was coming down a tree behind Mrs. Ross' chair. No one except Willy, that is.

"*Rowr rowr rowr rowr rowr!*" barked Willy suddenly, running under Mrs. Ross' chair.

83

"Oh!" cried Mrs. Ross, jumping up out of her seat.

The squirrel took off with Willy close behind—under bushes, through flowers, all around the garden.

"Willy, get back here," called Natasha halfheartedly.

No one could do anything but watch!

The animals turned and zoomed toward the group of chairs.

Suddenly, everything seemed to happen in slow motion.

The squirrel flung itself up toward the tree trunk, but didn't quite make it. It grabbed for the armrest of Mrs. Ross' chair, and then tumbled onto the table. Up flew a china dish and a bunch of cookies.

Mrs. Ross looked like she was screaming, but no sound came out.

Mr. Ross reached forward as the dish flipped over in the air. It landed neatly in his hand. His foot crunched several cookies.

"I saved it!" he cried.

Meanwhile the squirrel had scrambled off the table and up the tree trunk, with Willy yapping loudly below.

Mrs. Ross was so upset that her face was as pink as her dress.

"Thank you, David," she said, her voice shaking. "You saved the dish. Willy, go into the house right now. Natasha, take him inside. Excuse me, girls. I need to freshen up."

Molly wanted to clap. This was better than watching a movie!

Natasha got up slowly from her chair. As she passed the twins, they could see a hint of a smile on her face.

Don't laugh, don't laugh, don't laugh, Molly kept telling herself.

Amanda coughed. Only Molly knew that this was Amanda's way of hiding a chuckle.

Shawn, of course, knew what to do. She began to pick up the cookies from the ground. Molly and Amanda quickly began to do the same.

When Natasha came back outside, she looked more relaxed.

And when Mrs. Ross came back outside, she was holding a huge platter of delicious-looking cookies and pastries.

Amanda picked up a cream puff and popped it into her mouth. *This party won't be so bad after all,* she thought.

c h a p t e r

8

"**Y**ou should have seen it!" Molly told Peichi the day after the tea party. "That squirrel was so funny!"

The twins, Shawn, and Peichi were at Harry's, their favorite hangout in Park Terrace. They took turns filling Peichi in on the tea party.

"So then what happened?" asked Peichi. "After the squirrel went back up the tree?"

"Well, Mrs. Ross went inside for a moment. And she came out with more cookies, and then, here's the weird part—" Molly began.

"She acted like nothing funny or weird had happened!" Shawn broke in. "So we couldn't, either."

"We just talked some more, which was super boring, and then Natasha took us up to her room," added Amanda.

"*Oooh!* So, what's Natasha's room like?" Peichi wanted to know.

"You wouldn't believe it!" cried Molly.

"It looks like a princess's room in a castle," added Amanda as she bit into a roasted veggie wrap.

"She has the biggest bed. And it has white netting on top of it that she can pull down around her bed—" Shawn began.

"And there aren't any posters or anything like that on the walls," interrupted Molly. "Just oil paintings, and wall-paper, and drapes. It's pretty, but it doesn't look like a kid's room at all. She has a big old wooden trunk. But the best thing is the—how do you say it?"

"Chaise," said Shawn. "It's kind of a chair and a sofa together. With soft pink material. It's long, but it's not a sofa because on one side there's a chair back. It has one armrest. You can lie there and read a magazine like a movie star."

"Wow!" said Peichi.

"I thought the best thing was the walk-in closet!" exclaimed Amanda. "You walk right in the closet, and it's like another room! She has a dresser in there, and shelves, and shoe racks and little compartments...so cool."

"Peichi, are you mad at Natasha for not telling her mom to invite you?" asked Shawn as Peichi was about to take a bite of lemon-poppyseed cake.

Peichi shook her head. "Um, no, not really," she said uncertainly. She rested her elbow on the table, forgetting that her hand and fork were still in the air.

"Because I don't think Natasha really meant to leave you out," Shawn went on. She smiled and pointed at Peichi's fork. "Don't forget to eat your cake."

"*Oops*," giggled Peichi. She glanced at her pink plastic watch. "Oh, I have to go! I have to get home for my flute lesson." She gulped down the rest of her lemonade. "Harry's is so cool," she said, looking around. "I've never been here before. This is a lot better than Burger King!"

"Right, no screaming kids running around," said Molly. "It's our hangout—whenever we have some extra money."

The friends were the youngest people in Harry's, which made them feel cool. It was the kind of place where artists sketched and writers scribbled down their ideas. The place always smelled like fresh-brewed coffee, which it was famous for. The girls loved that smell, even though they couldn't stand the taste of coffee.

You could buy fruit smoothies, wraps of all kinds, and teas from all over the world. Hot tea came in funky old china teapots, and the cups never matched. Cookies were stored in big glass jars. Harry's hadn't always been a coffeehouse. A hundred years ago, it had been a drugstore. The dark wooden cabinets with glass shelves and sliding doors were still there, but Harry, the owner, had added little marble-topped tables and funky chairs. It was the perfect place if you were tired of plastic furniture, harsh bright lights, and greasy fast food.

"We'll walk you home, Peichi," said Amanda. That was the rule. Shawn's dad and the twins' parents had recently allowed them to roam Park Terrace without adults, but only if the girls stayed together. Peichi's mom had the same rule.

There was a lot to see and do in Park Terrace. Prospect

Park had a new zoo, an old carousel, a lake, an ice-skating rink, and softball fields. Park Terrace had pizzerias, bookstores, toy stores galore, and a puppet theatre. The huge library, art museum, and botanical gardens were great places to spend afternoons. And it was only a quick subway ride under the East River to Manhattan. New York City. The Big Apple.

"Hey, look! There's Justin," Molly said as they were walking down Seventh Avenue.

"Where?" exclaimed Amanda and Shawn.

Molly pointed to a boy in a ball cap who was with an older boy. "See? Over there? By the school. I think he's with his brother Ian. They're going to shoot hoops."

"Quit *pointing*, Molly!" cried Amanda. "Now he'll see us for sure."

"So?" asked Molly.

"So, we have to act like we don't see them," explained Amanda. "Duh!"

"What's your problem? Why should we hide from them? I mean, we cooked lots and lots of food for him and his entire family just a few weeks ago," said Molly, rolling her eyes. She and Peichi exchanged little smiles. Neither of them thought Justin was all that. Or any other boy, for that matter. As Peichi liked to say, "They haven't changed since the first grade. They're just a little taller."

"Let's cross the street so we can walk right by him," said Amanda.

"Well, then he's gonna see you!" said Peichi, giggling. Molly joined in, and she and Peichi began to really crack up. That annoyed Amanda even more.

"I'll cross with you," Shawn said.

All the girls ended up crossing the street. They headed toward the school, where Justin and Ian joined a group of kids playing basketball on the playground.

"C'mon, pass it! I'm wide open!" Justin was calling to someone.

Molly and Peichi were still giggling.

Amanda cleared her throat nervously. "*Sssh!*" she hissed to the friends. "Just act normal!" As the girls approached the wire fence of the playground, Amanda straightened her hot-pink sundress and started talking, just so Justin would think she didn't even see him.

There was only one problem. Justin didn't see Amanda. He was too much into the game.

Suddenly, Amanda pitched forward.

"Ow!" she cried.

Justin and all the other kids heard the cry and turned around just in time to see Amanda fall flat on her face!

The girls rushed to help her up.

"Are you okay?" they asked.

The sound of dribbling stopped. Justin and Ian started walking over near the fence.

No, no, don't come over now, thought Amanda as she looked down at her big toe. It was bleeding. "I'm all right," she said. "Come on, let's get out of here!"

But it was too late!

"Are you okay?" asked Justin. He stood a small distance from the fence, holding the basketball. His brown eyes looked concerned, but kind of confused, as if he was thinking, *How did she just fall over like that?*

"Oh, hi, Justin. Hi, Ian," said Amanda casually. The other girls just waved. They were too embarrassed for Amanda to even speak to the boys.

"I'm fine, I just tripped on something, I guess," said Amanda.

"Okay," said Justin, shrugging. "See you later."

"See you later," echoed Ian. They turned back to the game, and the boys started dribbling and shouting again.

Amanda led the group, walking away quickly. As soon as the girls were out of sight of the playground, she stopped.

"What happened back there?" asked Molly.

"I can't believe I fell down," wailed Amanda. She began to cry. "I stubbed my toe, and then I slipped on a pebble or something! Oh, I'm such a klutz! I can't ever look at Justin again! And I'm bleeding!"

"*Oooh,*" cried Molly. "There's a little flap of skin

hanging off your toe!" That made Amanda cry even more.

"Here, Amanda, I have a tissue," said Peichi.

"Don't worry, Manda. Justin won't think you're a klutz," Shawn assured her.

But Amanda was in a bad mood for the rest of the day, even though Mom and Molly pampered her with brownies and lemonade when the girls finally got home.

chapter 9

"Girls," said Mom the next morning as the Moores ate breakfast together, "have you decided what you're going to cook? We need to shop for the groceries after you both practice the piano."

"Molly and I talked about it last night," replied Amanda.

"We have a list, kind of," added Molly. She helped herself to another pancake. "These are so good, Dad." Dad didn't cook too often, but one of his specialties was blueberry pancakes from scratch. "Scratch" meant that it wasn't made from a mix.

"Can you make these for us next week, too, Dad?" asked Matthew. "I love them."

"That's why you're so quiet this morning," Dad teased Matthew. "You're busy eating my pancakes."

"We should feed him these every day, then," Amanda joked.

"Hey, you haven't asked me what *I* wanna eat next week when Mom's gone," Matthew told his sisters.

"Good point," said Mom. "What would you like the girls to make, Matthew?"

"*Hmmm.*" Matthew chewed and stared out into space.

"*Ssssh!* Matthew's thinking!" cracked Molly.

"I know, I can smell the smoke," added Amanda.

"Ha-ha, very funny," said Matthew. He was used to being teased by his big sisters. "Um, I want macaroni and cheese. And peanut butter cookies, and hamburgers, and pizza. But you guys can't make pizza, I guess."

"Why not?" asked Molly.

"Cause you have to get pizza from the pizza place."

"Actually, pizza is pretty easy to make," Mom told the kids.

Dad nodded. "I think you can make pizza dough ahead of time. Let's look at a recipe. Maybe we could have a little pizza party next week."

"Yeah!" cried Matthew excitedly. "Can Ben come?"

"That would be fun," said Molly. "Maybe Shawn could sleep over, too!"

"We'll talk about that later," said Dad. "Speaking of food for next week, remember that I'm going fishing tomorrow, so we'll have some tuna...I hope."

"Remember the last time you went fishing, Dad? You didn't catch anything, right?" asked Matthew.

"I remember, sport," said Dad. "But this time I'll catch a great big fish just for you!"

"Oops, we almost forgot the peanut butter," said Amanda as she checked the shopping list. She, Molly, and Mom were at Choice Foods, shopping for supplies for their cooking job.

"We can't forget the peanut butter for Matthew's cookies!" said Mom. "It's going to be fun to cook with you girls again. I really love that."

"We love it, too, Mom!" said Molly. "Oh, I'm going to miss you next week." She suddenly wanted to hug Mom, but that seemed weird, right in the middle of the supermarket aisle.

"Look," said Mom. "Isn't that Natasha coming in the door?"

"Yeah, and she's with her mom," said Amanda. "Oh good, you'll finally get to meet Mrs. Ross!"

"Now I'll see for myself what she's really like!" Mom said. "I'm sure she's a lot nicer than you girls make her out to be."

The twins waved to catch Natasha's attention.

"Hi!" Natasha called out, wheeling her shopping cart over. Her serious-looking face brightened up with a smile. "Hi, Mrs. Moore!"

The girls could smell Mrs. Ross' rose-scented perfume.

"Hi!" said the twins. "Hi, Mrs. Ross."

Mom and Mrs. Ross smiled at each other. "Hello," they said to each other.

"Mom, this is Mrs. Ross," said Amanda quickly. "Mrs. Ross, this is our mom."

Little Miss Manners strikes again, thought Molly. *Okay! I'm just jealous that I never know what to do!*

"How do you do!" said Mrs. Ross, shaking Mom's hand.

"Hello, I'm Barbara," said Mom.

"I'm Natalie."

For a split second, all was quiet. The girls put on big fat smiles and waited to hear what their moms would say.

"Well, my daughters had a wonderful time at your tea party the other day," Mom told Mrs. Ross.

"Yes, thank you, it was very nice," Molly spoke up. For once, she knew the right thing to say! *Score!* she thought. *I said something polite before Amanda did!*

"Thank you, Mrs. Ross," echoed Amanda.

"It was wonderful to have them!" Mrs. Ross exclaimed. "And Shawn, too. They're all such nice girls," she went on, "and Mr. Ross and I were very impressed with you all." She smiled at Molly and Amanda. "I hear you teach art history," said Mrs. Ross to Mom. "That's fascinating."

As Mom and Mrs. Ross began to chat, Natasha pulled the girls aside. "I'm not grounded anymore," she whispered. "Guess why."

"Why?" Amanda asked.

"They liked you all, and decided that I'm allowed to hang out with you. So they let me off the hook for sneaking out to cook with you."

"That's good," said Molly as low as she could. "Then come over and cook with us tomorrow. We're doing a bunch of cooking since Mom's going out of town. Okay?"

There she goes again, thought Amanda. *Who said I wanted Natasha to be there?*

"Okay!" said Natasha. Her blue eyes lit up. "I'll be there."

"...so nice to meet you, too," Mom was saying.

"Bye, girls," said Mrs. Ross.

Everyone said good-bye to each other, and Natasha and Mrs. Ross soon disappeared into the throng of shoppers and carts.

"Thanks a lot, Molly," said Amanda once the girls had helped put all the groceries away and gone up to their room.

"What? For what?" asked Molly. She was confused. What had she done now?

"Well, you just went ahead and told Natasha to come over tomorrow. Why didn't you ask me first?"

"Well, I never thought of asking you—" began Molly.

"That's just it! That's the problem!" Amanda began to shout. "You never think! You just go ahead and do it!"

"What's the *matter*, Amanda?" asked Molly, scrunching up her nose. "What are you talking about?"

"Now the money that Mom pays us isn't going to go as far, because we'll have to share it with Natasha."

Molly couldn't believe what Amanda was saying. "That's crazy, Amanda," she said. "You said yourself at Mom's party that Natasha could be one of the Chef Girls. So why can't she work on this job? Mom will pay Natasha herself—*we* won't have to pay her out of our money! You're not making any sense."

That comment made Amanda even angrier. "Well, why do you always just—just go ahead and say whatever you want?" she shouted. "You never ask me what *I* want!"

She stormed out of their room and went downstairs.

Molly fell back onto her bed and wondered why Amanda was always mad at her these days.

She talked to Mom about it later when Amanda was practicing the piano louder than usual. She was practically pounding the piano keys.

"Well, sweetie," said Mom as she began to brush Molly's hair, "I don't think this is about Amanda not wanting Natasha to come over tomorrow. I think she just wants you to talk to her first about the things you do together."

"Well, okay, I guess I don't always think to do that," said Molly. "But why does she always have to blow up at me? She's been so moody lately!"

Mom smiled at their reflection in the mirror. "You like to do things on the spur of the moment," she told Molly.

"But Amanda is like your dad. She has to consider every-thing! That's all. You two may be identical twins, but your personalities are very different. Just try to remember to include Amanda in your plans, that's all. Okay? I think that's fair. After all, your dad and I have to do that with each other."

"Okay, Mom," said Molly. "It's just that she never had a problem with me before. We used to always want to do exactly the same things."

"Maybe you really didn't, and now Amanda's sticking up for herself," said Mom. "See you downstairs, sweetie."

Maybe Mom is right, Molly thought. Molly had an idea. She grabbed a piece of Amanda's stationery, picked up a glitter pen, and wrote:

> Dear Amanda,
> I think I get it now. I'll make SUPER-sure to ask you what you want to do, when we're doing things together! Which is all the time! You're my best bud!
> Love, Molly

"I have a big announcement," Shawn told the twins later that night. The three of them had just watched a video and were sitting outside on Shawn's terrace. They liked hanging out there, above the rooftops of Park Terrace, on summer nights.

"What is it?" asked the twins.

"Is your dad going on that big trip?" asked Amanda.

"Actually, it's not an announcement. But I have an idea!" Shawn explained.

"What is it?" the twins asked again, giggling at "the twin thing."

"You know how we're always saying we don't have any money—" Shawn began.

"And it's so hard to make money," added Molly.

Shawn and Amanda shot each other a glance and started to giggle. They tried not to, but the harder they tried, the harder it was not to laugh.

Molly's face was getting redder and redder.

"Okay, go ahead and laugh," she said with a pout.

"Ha-ha! Sorry, Molls, but...ha! Ha-ha!" Amanda cracked up.

"Don't roll off the balcony," said Molly. She folded her arms across her chest and let out a big sigh.

Molly had tried having a pet-sitting service once, but she'd quit after only a few weeks. She'd had the worst luck a business owner could have. Even though she took very good care of all the pets, both Swishy the fish and Sam the hamster died while their owners were away.

The Weedons and the Wolfs blamed old age, not Molly. But after the hamster died, Molly decided to give up taking care of other people's pets.

"Anyway," said Amanda after her laugh attack was over, "it's not like there's a ton of baby-sitting to do, because there are so many nannies around here."

"Right!" said Shawn. "Well, tomorrow we're going to cook for your mom and get paid for it. Why don't we try to do that more often? Cook for people in the neighborhood? I mean, *our* parents aren't the only ones who don't have time to cook a real dinner every night."

Molly and Amanda looked at each other. Then they looked at Shawn.

"You mean, we'd have, like, a cooking *business?*" asked Amanda.

"Uh-huh!" said Shawn, smiling.

"How would we get customers?" asked Molly.

"We'd advertise," replied Shawn. "In the *Park Terrace Press.*"

"Does that cost money?" asked Amanda.

"Uh-huh."

"We could advertise for free all over Park Terrace," suggested Molly, "just by putting flyers up."

"That's true," said Shawn. "Anyway, I think it would be fun! We'd be making money just by hanging out together and doing something we like to do anyway."

"And working really hard," Amanda reminded her.

"I think it sounds pretty cool!" exclaimed Molly. "We could make so much money! Plus we would still cook for free sometimes, when people need help like the McElroys did."

Shawn nodded. "For sure," she said. "That was so great, helping people who didn't expect it."

Molly looked over at Amanda, who looked anxious, and said, "Well, we'll really have to think about it. Right, Manda?"

Amanda's face relaxed. She gave Molly a big smile. "Abso-*lute*-ly!"

To: happyface
From: mooretimes2
mooretimes2: howdy happyface!
happyface: Wei-wei mooretimes2!
mooretimes2: Wei-wei?
happyface: that means "hello" in Chinese!
mooretimes2: cool! wuzzup with u?
happyface: great! Ready 2 cook 2morrow with u! ☺
mooretimes2: groovy! We are psyched for Operation Feed the Moores and Get Paid.
happyface: what time?
mooretimes2: 2morrow morning at 10 or so.

Bring an apron ☺ We have something cool 2
talk to u about tomorrow!

happyface: :-@ what is it???? tell me NOW

mooretimes2: nope! It's a surprise. Sry, GTG,
Dad sez no more computer time 2nite ☹

happyface: ok. mwa**

mooretimes2: back at ya, L8R! <3 <3 <3

Molly and Amanda stayed up really late that night
playing "Crazy Eights" on the floor in their room.

"C'mon, Molls, just one more game," pleaded Amanda.
"Or we could play a different game. 'War.' Or 'Hearts.'"

"No way! I can't keep my eyes open," complained Molly.

"Oh, all right," said Amanda. She slid all the cards into
a pile and began to toss them up in the air.

"You're not mad at me again, are you?" asked Molly,
putting on her pj's, the ones with the moon-stars-clouds
print.

"No, why?" Amanda put the cards away in their box.

"Just checking...I hate it when you're mad at me,
Manda."

"So do I! I don't want to fight anymore. Anyway, good
night." Amanda threw on her leopard-print boy shorts and
tank top.

Click! She turned out the light.

"Hey! How's your big toe?" asked Molly, giggling in the dark.

"Just fine. Thanks for reminding me about the most embarrassing moment of my entire life! I thought you were tired."

"I was just tired of losing two games in a row! Hey, Amanda, what do you think of Shawn's idea?"

"Well, it's a good idea, but..."

"But what?"

"It sounds hard. Plus we're going to start middle school in the fall, and that's going to be hard, too."

"What do you think of having Natasha in the business?" asked Molly.

"That would be okay, I guess—the more people in something like this, the better. We would need all the help we can get!"

A car alarm went off outside.

"It would be nice to make money," Amanda continued with a yawn.

"What would you do with your money?" asked Molly. She was lying on her back, looking out the window. Tonight she had a view of a perfect crescent moon.

"Ida knooww, Molls...save up for something good-shhh..."

Amanda was out.

That was fast, thought Molly. She turned her head toward the window seat. It was upholstered in pale yellow velvet and had a collection of stuffed animals on it. She thought about getting out of bed to sit there and hold her stuffed elephant and watch the sky, but her legs refused to move.

As she stared up at the moon from bed, she thought about what she would do with the money she made. She could subscribe to magazines, buy more CDs, more cool sneakers...or would she save it? *Save it for what?* thought Molly. *A cool car! Yeah, like a Hummer. I'll be the only sixteen year-old with a Hummer, driving my friends around New York City...*

Molly was out.

chapter 10

The next day, Peichi was the first one over to start cooking.

"Hi, everyone! Hello, Kitty, don't run away from me! I brought some fresh basil from my mom's garden. What are we going to cook today? And what's the big thing you have to tell me? What do you want me to do first? Where's your mom?"

Peichi's shiny hair was up in a bun, with jeweled butterfly barrettes all around it.

"Your hair looks so cool!" cried Amanda. "I want you to do that to my hair."

"Sure," said Peichi. "It's so hot outside that I didn't want to even think about my hair. Are you guys going to come over and swim later?"

"I think so," Molly said. "If we get all this cooking done. We're going to make vegetable lasagna, pizza dough, my dad's favorite salad dressing, called Green Goddess, peanut butter cookies for Matthew, a Jell-O mold with fruit in it—"

"So, what's the big thing you wanted to tell me?" interrupted Peichi.

"Oh! Well, Shawn had this cool idea—" Molly began.

"But we haven't decided if we're going to do it or not," added Amanda.

"Right, because we have to think about it," said Molly.

"Because it's kind of a big deal," said Amanda.

"Well, what *is* it?" squealed Peichi. Everyone laughed.

"We could have a cooking business! You know, have our club, but cook for people in the neighborhood who are too busy to cook during the week."

"You mean we'd get paid?" asked Peichi.

"Uh-huh!"

"That is a great idea!" said Peichi.

"Yeah. We were over at Shawn's last night, and she told us about it."

"Oh," said Peichi. "Um, what did you do over at Shawn's?" She fiddled with a clip in her hair.

"Oh, we rented a movie, and just hung out," replied Amanda.

Peichi looked down at her sparkly blue toenails peeking through her sandals. "Why—why didn't you ask me to do that?" she asked.

Molly and Amanda looked at each other. *Uh-oh!* they both thought.

Molly cleared her throat. "Well," she said, not sure what to say next. "Shawn just called us, and said, 'What are you doing,' and we said, 'Nothing,' and she said, 'Come over and watch a movie, and my dad will make some popcorn.'"

Peichi kept looking down at her toenails.

Amanda spoke up. "You know, it was just a spur-of-the-moment kind of thing."

Peichi looked up. Her mouth quivered and her eyes filled with tears. "But I thought I was Shawn's friend, too," she said. "It sounds like she didn't even think to ask me to come over. And you didn't tell her to call me, did you?"

"Well," began Amanda.

"Um," said Molly. "It's just that, you know, we've known Shawn for a long time. We're like sisters to her. We helped her when her mom died. And—and—"

"And I guess sometimes we just don't think to ask anyone else to do something with us," Amanda added. "But it doesn't mean that we don't want to do things with you, Peichi!"

"Right," said Molly. "We really like you and always have so much fun with you. You know that."

Peichi sniffed. "I guess so," she said.

It seemed so strange to see Peichi crying!

"We didn't *mean* to leave you out," Molly assured Peichi. "Sometimes you want to do things with your other friends, and you don't think to invite us, right? That's okay!"

Peichi nodded. "Right," she said. "I just feel bad because Natasha didn't invite me to the tea party, and now this...it makes me wonder what's wrong with me?"

The twins smiled at Peichi. "Nothing's wrong with you!"

"We're glad you're our friend," Molly assured Peichi.

"And Shawn is, too," added Amanda.

"And Natasha, well, she's just—" began Molly.

Peichi smiled and said, "She's just Natasha!"

Everyone laughed. Peichi's smile seemed to fill up the kitchen. Both twins let out a sigh of relief.

"We're still friends, right?" Molly asked Peichi.

"Of course!" said Peichi. She put her arms around the twins. "I'm having a great summer with you guys."

"Well, anyway, think about this cooking business," said Molly.

"I'll have to ask my parents if I can do it," said Peichi.

"So will we," said Amanda. "So don't say anything about it in front of Mom today, okay?"

Just then, Mom came in from the backyard. She'd cut some of her deep pink roses.

"Hi, girls! Hi, Peichi!" she said. "Ready to cook?"

Bong! went the doorbell.

Shawn and Natasha had shown up at the same time.

"All the Chef Girls are here!" said Mom. "Great. I can help you get started, and then I have to run off to choir practice. I'll be back in a few hours to see how you're doing. Who wants to start the peanut butter cookies?"

"I will," said Natasha.

"Who wants to do the pizza dough?"

"Oh, I do!" cried Peichi.

"That'll take two people. Shawn, you can help her.

109

Molly and Amanda, you can make the salad dressing, and I'll help you do the lasagna later!" said Mom. "Okay?"

"You're the boss!" said Molly, and everyone cracked up.

"Do you ever just take a spoon and eat peanut butter out of the jar?" asked Amanda as Natasha measured half a cup of peanut butter.

"I thought I was the only one who did that!" said Natasha.

"No, all of us do that," said Amanda. "If our parents knew, they'd be totally grossed out."

"My grandmother used to make peanut butter cookies," said Natasha. "That's why I wanted to make them today. I don't remember Grandmother very well, though."

"Is that what you called her? 'Grandmother?'" asked Shawn.

"*Mmm-hmm.* She was old-fashioned. She hated 'Grandma.' She died when I was six."

"Do you have any other grandparents?" asked Shawn.

"No, they all died." Natasha looked up from her mixing bowl. "I wish I were more like all of you," she said to the girls.

Everyone stopped what they were doing.

"Um, what do you mean?" asked Amanda.

"Well, you know, more normal. I wish I had brothers and sisters—"

"I don't have any brothers or sisters," Shawn pointed out.

"Neither do I," said Peichi.

Natasha nodded. "Oh, right. Well, anyway, I just wish...well, never mind." She hid her face behind the cookbook, pretending to study her recipe.

No one said anything for a moment, but everyone was wondering the same thing: *What's the deal with Natasha?*

"So, Natasha, Shawn came up with this cool idea," Molly, changing the subject.

"We're thinking of starting a cooking business," Shawn continued, looking at Natasha and Peichi.

"I know about it," Peichi broke in.

"Oh. Well, anyway, Natasha, we'd cook for people in the neighborhood who are too busy to cook during the week."

"Like Mom!" said Molly.

"Wow!" said Natasha. "So, like, we'd do what we're doing today?"

"Uh-huh."

"It sounds good. And fun, too. But I'll have to ask my parents."

"So do all of us," said Shawn. "Let's talk to our parents in the next couple of days, and check back with each other."

Amanda put on a new CD and cranked it up, and the girls started working on their recipes.

Shawn and Peichi took turns kneading the pizza dough. It looked so fun that the twins and Natasha had to try it, too.

"How do we know when we don't have to knead it anymore?" asked Natasha as she placed her hands over the dough and began to press it.

"Um," said Peichi, reading over the recipe. "It says that the dough has to be smooth, but still moist. It should only take ten minutes or so."

"Then what do you do with it?" asked Molly.

"Then we put it in the fridge and let it rise for eight hours," said Shawn. "So don't forget to take it out later and put it in the freezer."

By the time Mom had gotten home from choir practice, the cooking session had turned into a party. The girls had made popcorn and were singing loudly along to the radio. Molly kept flipping from station to station, searching for their favorite songs and turning up the volume when she found them.

"Hi, Mom! The cookies are ready to go in the oven, and Amanda and I whipped up some pesto with Peichi's basil," reported Molly. "And we made the salad dressing, too."

"And the pizza dough is rising now," added Shawn.

"Good!" said Mom, reaching for the popcorn. "Let's start the lasagna. And we'll make an easy mustard sauce that you can use later. You'll just pour it over some chicken cutlets and bake them."

A few hours later, all the cooking was finished.

"My legs are sore!" exclaimed Peichi. "I have to sit down!"

"Have a seat," said Mom, gesturing toward the big kitchen table. "Let's all take a break and have some of these peanut butter cookies! Then we'll clean up the kitchen."

"Mmm," said Shawn as she bit into the soft cookie. "Too bad Matthew's not around! He's missing out!"

"We have to save him some," said Mom with a smile. "After all, we made these for him."

Just then, everyone heard the front door open. Matthew and Ben walked down the hall.

"Aw!" cried Matthew. "Why didn't you tell me!" He grabbed two cookies that were cooling on a wire rack and handed one to Ben.

"Hi, sweetie," said Mom. "Hi, Ben. They just came out of the oven. Do you want some milk?"

"*Mmph,*" replied Matthew, nodding.

"Hey, Matthew! We put mustard in them," teased Molly.

Matthew stopped chewing for a second, and he and Ben looked at each other.

"No, you didn't," replied Matthew with his mouth full. "These are good. Did you really make them?"

"Natasha made them," said Amanda. "Natasha, this is our brother Matthew and his friend Ben. You really didn't get to meet the other day."

Natasha smiled. "Hi," she said to the boys. The boys just sort of nodded. Matthew grabbed some more cookies, and the boys stomped through the kitchen, opened the storm door to the garden, and let it slam shut.

Peichi held her hands over her ears. "How come boys make so much noise?" she asked.

Molly turned to Natasha. "Matthew thinks he's really cool," she said. "Especially when he and Ben are together."

Natasha smiled. "Well, anyway, he liked my cookies," she said. She looked out the kitchen window. "He and Ben are wolfing them down out there!"

"I guess that means you should get paid now!" said Mom. She reached around the chair for her pocketbook. As she dug for her wallet, she smiled at the girls and said with a laugh, "Technically, you probably shouldn't get paid until you clean up the kitchen. But I'm going to trust you not to run off!" She pulled out several crisp green bills. "This is brand-new money out of the bank machine!"

"It looks fake, Mom," Molly teased her.

"Don't worry, it's the real thing. Here you go, Natasha,

thanks for doing such a great job on the cookies. And this is for you, Shawn. Here you go, Molly...and Amanda...and Peichi. Thank you."

"Thanks, Mrs. Moore!" said Peichi as she pocketed the money. "I *love* getting paid!" Everyone laughed.

"You've all done a great job, and now I feel better about going out of town. At least I know my family will be fed!" said Mom. "Now let's load up the dishwasher, 'cause I have to start tonight's dinner!"

The girls did such a great job cleaning up the kitchen that it didn't even look as if they'd been in there at all. Afterward, they all went upstairs to the twins' room with another plateful of peanut butter cookies and tall glasses of milk.

"I'm tired," said Shawn, falling back on Amanda's bed.

"Yeah, but it's a good kind of tired," said Natasha. She sat on the floor, leaned against Molly's bed, and looked around the room. "I like your room. It's big but cozy."

Amanda pulled her money out of her pocket. "I feel rich!" she said.

"So do I!" said Molly.

"I'm going to save my money," said Shawn.

"Not me," said Peichi. "Well, yeah, I guess I should save some of it."

"Actually," said Natasha, "this is the first time I've ever gotten paid. I want to do something special with the money."

"Like what?" asked Shawn, reaching for a cookie.

"I don't know...I'll think of something."

"Are we all going to talk to our parents tonight? About the business?" asked Molly, perched on her bed.

Everyone nodded.

"Great," said Shawn. "Let's all meet tomorrow and see what happened with everyone."

"Where should we meet?" asked Peichi. "Want to come over and swim?"

"You read my mind," Shawn replied with a grin.

chapter 11

That night, as the Moores finished dinner, Molly cleared her throat.

"Um, Amanda and I want to ask you something," she said. She told them about their idea for the cooking business.

Silence.

Mom and Dad looked at each other. Then they looked at the twins.

"A business?" asked Mom. "A *real* business?" She looked at Dad again.

Dad sighed and shook his head. "I don't know, girls," he said. "You're very new to cooking. You need adults around to help you. Have you really thought this out?"

"Sure," said Molly.

"A business needs capital," said Dad. "Where are you going to get that?"

"What's capital?" asked Amanda.

"Capital is the money that you need to start the business," explained Mom.

"You'll need money for groceries, advertising, and so on," said Dad.

"What would you call your business?" asked Mom. "You need a catchy name."

The twins looked at each other. "Dish," they said at the same time.

"Hmm, that *is* catchy," Mom said.

Molly and Amanda smiled.

"But a name is not everything. There's lots to think about when you start a business," Dad said.

"Oh, we'll figure things out," Molly said.

"Well, have you figured out how much you'd charge your customers?" asked Mom.

"Oh, well, um, we haven't really talked about *that* yet," replied Molly.

"Most importantly, girls, what are you really selling? Tell me what your business is about," said Dad.

"Well," said Amanda, "we would cook food for people who are too busy to cook."

"So, what does that mean?" asked Dad. "How much food would you cook? Is it for one meal? More than one meal?"

"Oh, it would have to be for more than one meal," said Molly. "We'd do like what we did for the McElroys and for Mom. Like a whole bunch of meals."

"But how many meals exactly?" asked Dad. "You need to decide, because that's what your business would be about. That's what you'd put in your ad. You need to say, 'We'll cook five nights' worth of dinners and deliver it to you,' or whatever."

"It would have to be five days, I guess," said Amanda. "So that people know that they don't have to cook dinner for one whole workweek."

Matthew rolled his eyes. "Can I please be excuuuuu-used?" he asked. "This is so *boring!*"

Mom nodded, and Matthew got up from the table.

"How would you deliver the food?" asked Dad.

"You girls *cannot* cook every day," said Mom, "especially once school starts. You have cooking classes and piano lessons. Plus you're starting middle school soon! You'll have to get adjusted to that. And there will be after-school activities you want to do there, I hope."

Molly and Amanda looked at each other.

"Plus," said Dad, "where would you do the cooking? Our house? Or would you take turns at the other girls' houses? That's something we need to talk about. Maybe your mom and I don't want a cooking business going on here all the time."

"It could be disruptive, girls," Mom said gently. "And you'd also need to think about where you would store the food. There wouldn't be room to store it in our refrigerator. You'd need to keep it separate, anyway, so we wouldn't use it by mistake. I think it's great that you have your cooking club," Mom continued with a big smile, "and that you're helping me out so much. But I think you should just leave it at that for a while."

Molly's head was starting to spin. She felt a huge lump growing in her throat. *Don't cry now!* she told herself. She was mad at Mom and Dad, but deep down, she also knew they were right. *We haven't thought this out at all,* she admitted to herself.

She sneaked a look at Amanda. Amanda didn't look upset. But she did look a little dizzy.

Dad pushed his chair back from the table. "I'm sorry, girls, but we'll have to talk about this at another time," he said. "After you've thought out your idea more."

Mom smiled sympathetically at the girls. The twins tried to smiled back.

"Your dad's right," said Mom. "Well, I need to starting packing for my trip now. You'll help Dad do the dishes, won't you?"

"So, how did it go with your dad?" Molly asked Shawn the next day.

The twins and Shawn had met up at a bench facing the Prospect Park lake to walk over to Peichi's together.

"Well, he asked me a lot of questions," replied Shawn. "And I didn't know how to answer them!"

"Our parents asked us a million questions, too," said Amanda. "Hey, what's that?" She pointed to something very tiny and black. It was beginning to cross the road that ran through the park.

"It's a big bug!" cried Molly.

"*Aw*, it's a baby turtle!" cried Shawn.

"How cute!" said Molly, leaning over it. "Don't cross the road, little turtle, or you'll get squashed."

Amanda picked up the turtle. It was so small that it fit in the palm of her hand. "Poor little thing, he's all mixed up. Are you scared? Don't worry, I'll put you back near the water. Your mom's looking for you." She looked around. "I wonder where he came from?" she asked.

Shawn pointed to a tree limb that jutted out of the water right by the edge of the lake. "The turtles live over there," she said. "Dad and I saw them come out of the water one day and sun themselves on that big branch. There were about fifteen of them! Let's set him there. Can I carry him now?"

"So we did our good deed of the day," said Amanda, as she told Peichi and Natasha about the tiny turtle.

"That little turtle was lucky," said Peichi. "Hey, I have something to show you."

The friends had just gotten to Peichi's and were in her room. Peichi opened her closet door and brought out the dress her mom had bought for Peichi to wear in an upcoming family wedding. It was pale pink silk, long, and sleeveless.

"*Oooh*, you're going to look so good in it!" cried Amanda. "Model it for us!"

"Okay!" said Peichi. She was unzipping the plastic garment bag when Mrs. Cheng called from her office, "Peichi, leave that dress in the bag, please! I don't want you to wrinkle it before the wedding!" Mrs. Cheng worked at home. Her office was down the hall from Peichi's room.

"Okay, Mom!" called Peichi. She turned to her friends. "My mom hears *everything!*" she said in a loud whisper. "How does she do that?"

"Oh, well, let's go outside," Molly suggested. Peichi hung up the dress and closed the closet door, and the girls went outside to the pool.

"I talked to my mom and dad about the business," said Peichi, as she poured soda into tall glasses full of ice. "It didn't go so well! They asked me all kinds of questions! They said I was just learning how to cook! They said I have too much going on, like flute lessons and stuff! And then they said, 'Not right now.' Then I got kind of upset, and they said they'd think about it."

"Do you know what my dad said?" asked Shawn. "He said, 'If you start working now, you'll be working the rest of your life.' I was like, 'So? What's wrong with that?' And then he laughed at me and said I'd figure it out someday!"

The twins nodded.

"This sounds familiar," Molly remarked, glancing at Amanda. "It didn't go so well at our house, either."

"Gee, I guess I'm the only one whose parents actually liked the idea," said Natasha.

"Get outta here!" exclaimed Shawn.

"*Your* parents?" cried Peichi and the twins. They couldn't help laughing, and Natasha laughed, too.

"Yeah, believe it or not!" replied Natasha. "My dad said it would be a really good experience for me. Even my mom thought it sounded like fun. But they both said my schoolwork had to come first."

Molly folded her arms across her chest and looked at her friends. "You know," she said, "my dad brought up a lot of stuff that we never really thought about. I mean, you have to admit, we didn't talk about how we'd run the cooking service, like where we'd keep the food—"

"What we'd cook—" Amanda broke in.

"All that kind of stuff," continued Molly. "Plus we don't have any—what's it called? Capital."

"Hey! My dad used that word, too," said Peichi with a giggle.

"So did mine!" said Shawn.

"So did mine," said Natasha. "But guess what! I couldn't wait to tell you. My dad offered us the money—I mean the capital—to get started!"

"Really?" cried the girls all at once.

123

"Really," replied Natasha. "So, if we really want to do this, we can."

"That's so cool!" cried Molly.

Natasha tucked her hair behind her ears and cleared her throat. "The thing is," Natasha went on, "we'd have to pay him back. We could pay him back a little at a time. He said that's how it works in the real world. If you want a bank to loan you money, you have to pay it back. He'd be, like, our bank."

"Okay, that sounds fair," said Shawn, nodding her head.

"We could do that," added Peichi.

"Plus he said he won't charge us interest," added Natasha.

"What's interest?" asked the twins.

"It's a fee you have to pay for borrowing money," Natasha explained. "My dad told me that whenever you take out a loan, like, for a house or a car, the bank charges you interest. But my dad isn't going to do that!"

"That's really great," said Amanda. "But we still have a lot to work out."

"Well, we have a refrigerator in our garage," said Peichi, pointing her carrot stick at the garage door. "There's not much in it. We keep sodas in there, and the turkey at Thanksgiving, stuff like that. We could store the food there, at least sometimes. But I'd have to ask to make sure. Sometimes it's full."

Shawn shrugged. "Don't look at me," she said. "I'm the

only one here who lives in an apartment. Dad and I don't have room to store extra food."

Natasha excitedly waved a potato chip in the air. "Maybe we could buy our own refrigerator! I'll bet we could keep it in my basement!"

Everyone laughed really hard at the idea of the friends shopping for a refrigerator together.

"But Natasha's right," said Shawn. "That way, we'd never have to deal with asking our parents, 'May we please store our food in your fridge?' Our stuff would never be in the way. It would free us up."

Everyone nodded.

Amanda snapped a pretzel stick in half. "Fridges are expensive," she pointed out.

"We don't have to buy a new one, silly," said Molly. "We'd buy a used one at a tag sale."

"Or from a newspaper ad," Peichi added.

"Whoa!" said Shawn. "We don't have to worry about that right now! We'd only have to do that if business was really good!"

"That's true," said Peichi. "We have a lot of other things to worry about before we get to that point!"

"And Amanda and I came up with a cool name for the business. Dish!" Molly said.

"That's a *great* name!" Shawn said. "I love it!"

The rest of the girls agreed, too.

125

"So what do we do now?" asked Amanda.

"We go back to our parents and say, 'Guess what! We have *capital*, and we're not being charged *interest*,'" said Peichi with a laugh. "They're gonna be so surprised! Come on, let's jump in the pool!"

"You got sunburned here," Amanda told Molly later that day as they looked through a magazine together in their room. She gently poked Molly's upper arm.

"*Ow*," said Molly. "I guess I forgot the sunscreen there...so, what do you think of Dish, the business? Are you into it? I can't really tell what you're thinking."

Amanda looked thoughtful. "It could be fun," she replied. "We'd all be together, making money. I—I'm into it. I guess."

"Then the question is, can we get Mom and Dad to let us try it," said Molly.

"I think that's what we have to say," said Amanda, nodding. "We'll ask if we can just *try* it! And if it doesn't work out, no big deal."

"Capital? You got capital from Mr. Ross?" asked Dad

that night as the Moores lingered in the garden after dinner. He slapped at a mosquito.

"Uh-huh. And Mr. Ross isn't going to charge us any—"

"Interest," Amanda broke in.

"Right, interest," continued Molly, as she threw Amanda a grateful look. "And we all talked about the business today at Peichi's, and we came up with some good ideas on how to run it."

"Like, what we would cook," said Amanda. "We decided that if someone calls and wants a week's worth of meals, we'll just tell them what we're cooking that week. We won't really take requests. That would get too complicated, and we wouldn't be able to shop in advance."

"Really, we just want to give it a try," said Molly. "Can't we just try it and see if we can even do it?"

Mom nodded her head thoughtfully. She looked at Dad, and Dad nodded. The twins knew this was a good sign.

"We'll think about it," said Dad. "Sorry, girls, that's the best we can do for now."

"We'll let you know soon," said Mom.

But I want to know now, thought Molly.

The twins knew to let the matter be for now, even though Mom was flying to San Diego in the morning.

"Oh! The suspense is killing me!" Molly told Amanda as they went upstairs. They didn't really feel like staying with Mom and Dad in the garden after their talk.

Amanda flipped on the light in their room. "At least we'll still have our cooking club, and who knows—maybe Mom and Dad will say yes!"

Molly dived on to her bed, and hugged Mumbles, her old teddy bear. "What if everyone else is allowed to do the business except us?" she groaned. "That would be horrible!"

"Don't worry, Molls," said Amanda coolly, as she lifted a clean pair of pj's out of a drawer. "That'll never happen."

"**G**ood-bye, girls," said Mom early the next morning, clutching the twins close. "Bye, Matthew." She kissed Matthew, who made a face.

Outside, the taxi driver honked. "I'm coming!" Mom called out the door, waving. "Where's my purse? Be good for Dad, okay? I've put my hotel phone number here on the fridge—"

"We know, Mom, you showed us three hundred times," said Matthew.

"Bye, Mom!" chorused the twins.

Molly went into the kitchen and sleepily poured cereal into a bowl. The phone rang.

"Hi, Amanda?"

"Hi, Peichi, it's Molly. You're up early!"

"Oh, hi, Molly! So are you! Guess what! My parents are going to let me try the business! At least for the summer. But they said if it gets to be too much with school in the fall, I have to quit! But isn't it great? Did you talk to your parents yet? What did they say?"

Molly explained to Peichi what had happened when she and Amanda spoke to their parents last night. Still no news.

121

"Well, as they say: 'no news is good news,'" Peichi said as she hung up the phone.

As soon as Molly put down the receiver, the phone rang again.

"I'll get it this time," Amanda said grabbing the phone.

"Hello? Hi, Shawn...not much. Mom left this morning. What's up with you?...Oh, really? Your dad is letting you do the business? Wow. Peichi's allowed, too...Well, we still don't know yet!"

"Matthew! Come on in! It's time for lunch," Amanda called out the door later that day. Matthew was skating up and down the hill.

"It's about time!" he called back. "What are we having?"

"Just come on in and find out."

As the twins and Matthew ate peanut butter-and-honey sandwiches, the phone rang. As usual, Amanda was the first to grab it.

"Hello? No, Mrs. Moore isn't here right now...yes, this is her daughter Amanda...right, we cooked for the McElroys after they had their fire...*Mmm-hmm*...I think that would be okay, but I'll have to talk it over with my friends. Can I call you back?" She wrote down a phone number. "Okay. Thank you. Bye."

Amanda hung up the phone and looked at Molly, her eyes wide.

"Who was that?" asked Molly and Matthew at the same time.

"Someone named Mrs. Freeman. She's a friend of Mrs. McElroy, who told her about our cooking. Mrs. Freeman asked if we would cook a bunch of dinners for her family. She has to go take care of her sick mother in another state. And she offered to pay us a lot of money!"

"Wow," said Molly. "It's like our business is happening without us even trying!"

"Don't you think we should check with Mom and Dad first?" Amanda said. "I mean, they haven't really given us permission to start our business yet."

"Then this is our perfect opportunity!" Molly said. "If we do a good job, we can prove to them that we can do the business."

Amanda twirled a piece of her hair around her finger. "I don't know, Molly. We'll need a place to cook, plus we'll need a parent to help us deliver the food. We just can't carry it all on our bikes!"

Molly sighed. "You're right." She picked up the phone and dialed Dad.

After Molly explained what was going on, their dad agreed to let them cook. He said they could take it on a "case-by-case basis."

Molly and Amanda were psyched!

"Let's call the others," said Amanda.

Molly and Amanda called Peichi and Shawn and arranged to cook the next weekend. They left a message on Natasha's family's answering machine.

Later that day, as the twins, Peichi, and Shawn hung out at Peichi's pool, they talked about all the dishes they would cook.

"Pesto's always easy," Shawn pointed out.

"And we can use the basil from my mom's garden," Peichi pointed out.

"But we still need money to buy ingredients for the rest of the food," Amanda said. "Since we don't have our *capital* yet!"

"I haven't spent the money that your mom paid us," said Peichi as she floated in the water. "Believe it or not!"

Neither had anyone else.

"Is Natasha coming over today?" asked Molly. "She never called us back."

"She didn't call me back, either," said Peichi.

Amanda rolled her eyes. *Typical,* she thought.

A few days later, it was time to cook for Mrs. Freeman. The girls decided to meet early in the morning at the Moore's and go to Choice Foods together. Peichi and Shawn showed up on time.

"Is Natasha here yet?" asked Peichi.

"No," said Molly. "We left her a message that we were going shopping, but we still haven't heard from her."

The girls waited around for a while, then called her house. There was no answer.

"Let's just go," said Amanda. She sounded annoyed. "Maybe she'll call while we're out, or just meet us at the store."

There was no message from Natasha when the girls returned from the store, loaded down with bags. "Is she coming or not?" Amanda said, looking at the phone. "We need her. There's a ton of work to do." She looked at the food they'd just bought. It was all over the kitchen, and as she always did, she thought, *How are we going to cook all this food?* The girls were going to make pesto, a Jell-O mold, cucumber-and-dill soup, chocolate chip cookies, a pasta salad, a three-bean salad, a mustard sauce for baking chicken breasts, a vegetable lasagna...

The girls had arranged with Mrs. Freeman to make enough food for six dinners. They had to do it all in one day, because Mrs. Freeman asked if they could bring the food over a day earlier than she'd originally needed it. And Mom wasn't around to help! Dad would be around, but he'd already committed to playing golf and wouldn't

133

be back until the afternoon. Luckily, he let the girls start cooking without him, since he was beginning to feel more comfortable about them using the kitchen by themselves.

The girls weren't as talkative as usual, and no one turned the radio on for a while. Amanda finally brought up what everyone else was thinking. "Where's Natasha? Why hasn't she called?"

"Don't worry, Manda, she'll be here," said Molly as she chopped some herbs, but she didn't sound very confident.

"How do you know?" retorted Amanda. "This business isn't going to happen if we have to rely on *her!*"

Peichi and Shawn sneaked each other a glance that said, *Uh-oh!*

"I'm tired of always wondering what's going on with Natasha, Natasha, Natasha!" said Amanda crossly. "We never really know if she's going to show up or not, and something's always weird about her."

"That's not very nice," retorted Molly. She set down her knife and put her hands on her hips.

Shawn and Peichi tried to look as though they were completely fascinated with washing vegetables and spinning them dry in the salad spinner.

With a loud clatter, Amanda threw some metal measuring spoons on the counter, walked out of the kitchen, and stomped upstairs.

No one said anything. The kitchen suddenly seemed

huge to Peichi. The whirring salad spinner seemed too loud.

Shawn cleared her throat. She hadn't seen the twins argue in a long time, and she wasn't sure what to do.

Molly sighed. "She'll be back," she said, and went to turn on the radio. The music helped.

Sure enough, a few minutes later, Amanda came back downstairs. "Shawn," she said in a low voice, "can you ask Molly where she put the chocolate chips?"

Shawn looked at her for a moment, surprised. She shrugged as if to say, *Why don't you just ask her yourself?* But Amanda just looked steadily at her as if to say, *Do it!*

"Um, Molly, Amanda wants to know where you put the chocolate chips," said Shawn.

Molly didn't say anything for a moment. Then she leaned down, pulled the bag of chocolate chips out of the cupboard, and set them on the counter. Shawn picked up the bag and took it over to Amanda.

A little while later, Molly said, "Peichi? Would you please get the mustard out of the refrigerator?"

Peichi looked up, surprised. She was the farthest away from the fridge. Amanda was working next to it.

"Oh, sure," said Peichi, walking quickly over to the fridge. "Um, excuse me, Amanda, I need to just—get—in here. Thanks." She practically trotted the mustard over to Molly, who primly said, "Thank you."

135

Shawn rolled her eyes. Boy, was it a pain when the twins weren't getting along.

Dad was a big help with the lasagna when he got home, and everyone was glad he was in the kitchen. Dad was always a little bit in his own world, so he didn't even notice that the twins weren't speaking to each other. This was a good thing. It helped make everything seem a bit more normal.

Finally, after what seemed like two days instead of one, all the food was ready, and everyone began to pack it up and put it into boxes. Luckily, at the store Shawn had thought to buy inexpensive plastic food storage boxes that Mrs. Freeman could keep.

Dad offered to drive the girls over to the Freemans', who lived just a few blocks away, on his way to pick up Matthew from soccer practice. The girls carefully set the boxes in the trunk. Amanda phoned Mrs. Freeman to tell her they were on their way, and then everyone piled in the car.

It took only a few minutes to get to Second Street.

"You go first, Dad," said Molly, handing him a box.

Dad shook his head. "Uh-uh, Molly. This is *your* business, not mine."

Molly marched up the stairs and rang the bell. Mrs.

Freeman answered the door with a friendly smile. Her short, stylish black hair was streaked with gray, and she wore jeans and a glittery T-shirt just like the girls did.

"Hi!" said Mrs. Freeman. "I'm Carol!"

"Hello, I'm Molly. And this is Amanda, Peichi and Shawn. And my dad."

The girls had fun showing Mrs. Freeman everything they'd made.

"It all looks great," she said. "I know my husband and daughters will love it. Thank you. Here's your money. I'll give it to you, dear." She handed a big wad of bills to Shawn.

Shawn almost began to count the money, but decided that it might look rude, as if she didn't trust Mrs. Freeman. So she stuffed it in the pocket of her orange board shorts.

"Thank you!" chorused the girls. And that was it. They followed Dad out the door, said good-bye to Mrs. Freeman, and turned to walk home.

"Do you want me to drive you back?" asked Dad.

"No, that's okay," said Molly. "It's good to be outside."

"Okay, see you in a few minutes." Dad got in the car and headed off to pick up Matthew.

"We did it!" Peichi cried jumping up and down. "Our first, I mean, second job!"

"Let's divvy up the money," Molly said, poking Shawn. "I can't wait to get my hands on it!"

Amanda stopped walking. "Shawn, will you please tell

my sister that it's not a good idea to count your money in the middle of the street!"

Molly rolled her eyes. Amanda was still mad at her.

"Oh my *gosh!*" cried Peichi. "It's Natasha!"

"Where?" asked Shawn.

"See? Way up the street? She's walking her dog."

"No way! Forget about her! I'm not in the mood to see her right now," Amanda snapped.

"Me neither," said Shawn. "Let's turn around and go up Third Street instead."

"Well, I want to talk to her!" Molly said. "I want to find out what's going on!"

"Me too," said Peichi. "I'll go with you, Molly."

"We'll see you guys back at the house," Molly told Amanda and Shawn. They looked at each other and shrugged. "Okay," they said, and turned down the street.

Molly and Peichi walked quickly to catch up to Natasha.

 "Hey, Natasha," called Peichi. Natasha stopped walking, her back to Molly. She slowly turned around to face her.

"Hi, Natasha," said Molly. "Hi, Willy!" Willy began to jump up excitedly.

"Hi," said Natasha. She looked almost afraid.

"What's up? How come you didn't return our calls?" asked Molly. She hoped her voice didn't sound too mean.

"Sorry," said Natasha. "Um—sorry."

"Is everything okay?" asked Peichi.

"Um, yeah. Well, it's just that I can't bring the capital now. Okay?"

"O-kay," said Molly slowly.

"I'll talk to you later," said Natasha.

"Bye," said Molly and Peichi as they watched Natasha turn around. But then Molly began to feel really angry.

"Natasha? Wait a minute. Did your dad change his mind?" asked Molly.

Natasha stopped and said, "No, not really."

"Come on, Natasha. We're your friends. If you want friends, you have to be honest with them!" Molly said. "You completely blew us off today, and we're not sure if you're in this cooking thing with us or not."

"You can tell us," added Peichi.

Natasha looked up. Willy waited and panted, staring at Molly and Peichi with his big, round eyes. Finally, Natasha looked at the two of them and said, "My dad lost his job, okay? So there's no capital now. He probably would've still given it to me, but I didn't want to take it. Okay? That's it. Blame me, not him. I'm sorry. Come on, Willy." She turned away.

"It's okay, Natasha!" called Molly.

"Do you still want to cook with us?" called Peichi, but Natasha never looked back.

139

chapter 13

When Molly and Peichi got back to the Moore's, they told Amanda and Shawn what had happened.

"That's sad," said Shawn. "It must be kind of scary when your dad loses his job."

"I feel sorry for her and all," Amanda said, "but give me a break—why are we spending so much time thinking about Natasha?"

No one said anything.

"Well!" said Peichi, finally. "Um, Shawn, do you have something to give us?"

Everyone giggled as Shawn took the money out of her pocket. "I sure do!" she said. She passed out all the money.

"Let's see," said Peichi, doing math in her head. "We definitely made a profit, because this is more than we spent on the groceries. *Woo-hoo!*"

"I think we should celebrate!" said Molly. "Let's do something fun with this money."

"Like what?" asked Amanda. It was the first time she'd really spoken to Molly in hours.

"How about having a party at my house? I'll ask my mom if we can do it tomorrow night," suggested Peichi.

"We'll have a sleepover! And you'll get to see the pool at night, all lit up. It's so pretty!"

"We could order a gigantic hero," added Shawn. "You know, one of those three-foot long things."

"That sounds like fun," said Molly.

"Listen guys," Amanda said. "Sorry I was in such a bad mood today. It's just that I was worried we couldn't do everything. But it all turned out okay!"

"That's right," said Molly. "Because we all worked together, and because Dad was nice enough to help us." She giggled. "Our house is going to be quiet tomorrow night! It'll just be Dad and Matthew here."

The next evening, the twins and Shawn walked over to Peichi's together.

They had just dumped their stuff in Peichi's room when the doorbell rang.

"Oh, that's probably the food!" said Peichi. The girls followed her to the front door.

"DiMaggio's Heroes. You ordered a six-foot hero?" asked the pimple-faced delivery boy.

Peichi's eyes opened wide, and inside the living room the other girls began to giggle.

"Six feet!" she cried. "No, we ordered a *three*-foot hero!" she cried. "Oh, no! You guys got it wrong!"

The boy looked confused and checked the receipt.

"I'll have to get my mom—" began Peichi.

"That's okay," said the boy. "Our mistake. This does say "Three feet." I'll just charge you for the three-foot sub, okay? But you can keep the whole thing. Plus all the sides that come with it."

 "The whole thing!" exclaimed the girls. What were they going to do with a six-foot long hero?

"Well, bring it in!" said Peichi. "I'll help you!"

The friends couldn't stop laughing as they watched Peichi help the boy haul in a hero that looked as if it could feed a hundred people.

"Thanks," said Peichi to the boy as he left. "And here's a tip."

"Thank you!" said the boy. "Good luck with that hero!"

"I think we should call some more people!" said Peichi. She went to find her mom.

Mrs. Cheng came in from the garden. "Oh, no!" she cried. "It's huge! Well, I'll forget about cooking dinner! Your dad and I will help you eat this. Girls, call your parents and let's have a bigger party!"

That's what everybody did. Soon all the girls' parents were on their way, plus Matthew and Ben!

The girls went out to the pool to wait for everyone to come.

"Okay!" said Shawn, jumping to her feet. "I can't wait

any longer!" Shawn was usually so cool, but right now she looked as if she had a huge secret. "I got an e-mail from Grandma Ruthie today," she said. "Grandma Ruthie with a capital R!"

The friends looked at each other, confused.

"Grandma Ruthie with a capital R!" repeated Shawn. "Don't you get it? *Capital?*"

"Oh!" cried Amanda. "Does this mean—"

"That your grandma is going to give us capital?" Peichi broke in.

Shawn nodded, her eyes bright.

"*Yes!*" said Molly. "Oh, now our parents *have* to let us, Manda!"

"You know that my grandma loves to cook, and she's excited that *I'm* learning to cook now. She offered the money. I didn't even ask her!" Shawn explained.

"All right!" exclaimed Molly. She high-fived Shawn. The girls were psyched!

Soon everyone's parents were there. The girls helped Mr. and Mrs. Cheng bring out ice, soft drinks, and paper plates.

After a while, Molly and Amanda cornered Dad.

"...and so Grandma Ruthie has come up with the capital," Molly explained. "Dad, we really want to try this.

Can we just see how it goes? Please? Everybody else is allowed! And Peichi thinks we can store the food in their extra fridge, but we won't even have to *worry* about that for a while!"

"Well," said Dad after he swallowed a big bite of his hero, "you girls did very well yesterday. And it would be a good way to learn about managing money. You still haven't worked out all the details, and your mom's not here to put in her vote, but I think she'll agree with me that for now, we'll look at it as a summer job. You just can't get behind on your piano lessons, okay?"

"*Yessss!*" cried Molly and Amanda, high-fiving each other. They ran off to tell the others.

Everyone was really getting along well at the party. Molly and Amanda looked around at their friends and everyone's parents. They were all standing around the glowing blue pool, chatting away while they balanced soggy paper plates. The warm evening went on and on, but it seemed to Molly and Amanda as if their summer had just begun. And what a summer it was going to be!

The Amazing Cookbook

By

The CHEF Girls

AMANDA!

Molly!

Peichi ☺

shawn!

Hot Dogs!

there are lots of ways to make good hot dogs. Here are two!

"REGULAR" HOT DOGS

1) Bring a pot of water to a boil, then turn off the heat.

2) Place hot dogs in the water for 10 minutes.

3) Remove them with tongs and put them in hot dog buns. the Moore kids like their buns toasted in the toaster oven,

Shawn likes hers un-toasted, and of course Peichi likes them either way!

4) serve with mustard (gotta have mustard!); ketchup; relish; chopped onion; Dad likes sauerkraut on his; Mom eats only mustard and onion on hers, she says that's the real New York way!

My friend Crystal, who lives in chicago, puts mustard, relish, a pickle spear, chopped tomato, 2 whole hot peppers (some people take them off but the taste stays), cubed raw onion, and a dash of celery salt on hers! It's not just Crystal who does that. She says that's how most people eat hot dogs in chicago. they sure put a lot of stuff on them.

—shawn

FANCY GRILLED HOT DOGS

this is how Dad makes them when he's the chef. Make sure an adult is with you at the grill!

1) Make a few gashes in the hot dog with a knife.

2) Grill it until you see grill marks on the hot dog.

3) put some cheddar cheese and grated onion in the gashes and wrap a cooked bacon strip around the hot dog. Dad quickly toasts the buns on the grill, too.

You will be the star of the picnic!

147

CARMEN'S BISCOTTI

PREHEAT OVEN TO 325 DEGREES.

YOU WILL NEED:

PARCHMENT PAPER (to put on cookie sheets, you don't
have to have it, but it will make it easier to take cookies
off cookie sheets. you can get it in the grocery store.)

3/4 CUP ALMONDS, CHOPPED

1/2 CUP BUTTER, OR A LITTLE LESS

1 CUP SUGAR

2 EGGS

1 TABLESPOON ANISE EXTRACT

1 1/2 TEASPOONS ANISE SEEDS

1 1/2 TEASPOONS BAKING POWDER

1/2 TEASPOON SALT

2 CUPS FLOUR

1/3 CUP YELLOW CORNMEAL

POWDERED SUGAR

1. USE AN ELECTRIC MIXER TO CREAM TOGETHER THE BUTTER AND SUGAR UNTIL COMBINED.
2. THEN BEAT IN THE EGGS ONE AT A TIME, ANISE EXTRACT, BAKING POWDER, AND SALT.
3. NOW STIR IN THE FLOUR, CORNMEAL, ALMONDS, AND ANISE SEEDS.
4. TURN OUT ONTO SLIGHTLY FLOURED BOARD AND KNEAD TO COMBINE (THIS IS THE FUN PART!). IF THE DOUGH IS STICKY, ADD MORE FLOUR, A LITTLE AT A TIME.
5. NOW FORM THE DOUGH INTO 2 LOGS AND PLACE ON COOKIE SHEET, ON TOP OF PARCHMENT PAPER.

(IF YOU DON'T USE PARCHMENT PAPER, THEN BUTTER THE COOKIE SHEETS AND DUST THEM WITH FLOUR INSTEAD.)
6. BAKE UNTIL GOLDEN BROWN (25 MINUTES OR SO). BRING OUT AND SLIDE OFF ONTO CUTTING BOARD VERY CAREFULLY. SLICE THE LOGS INTO 2-INCH SLICES, THEN LAY THE SLICES SIDE-WAYS ON COOKIE SHEET AND BAKE ANOTHER 10-15 MINUTES.
7. PUT THE COOKIES ON RACKS. THEN DIP EACH SLICE IN POWDERED SUGAR TO COAT. STORE IN AN AIRTIGHT CONTAINER AFTER COOLING, AND THEY'LL LAST A FEW WEEKS!

YUM!

149

Carmen's "Chicken under a Brick"

This recipe comes from the town of Lucca, in a region called Tuscany.
Carmen says that Tuscany is in northern Italy and is very beautiful.
An adult will need to help you lift the skillet!

You will need 2 heavy ovenproof skillets; one needs to fit into the other
1 whole chicken, split (or butterflied), with the backbone removed.
Have the butcher at the supermarket do this for you.
1 tablespoon minced fresh rosemary leaves
or 1 teaspoon dried rosemary
1 teaspoon dried tarragon leaves
2 teaspoons salt
½ teaspoon pepper
1 tablespoon garlic, chopped
2 tablespoons olive oil

1. Make the marinade by mixing the rosemary, garlic,
   salt, pepper, and 1 tablespoon of the olive oil
   over the chicken. Put it under the skin, too.
   Refrigerate for at least a few hours, or up to 24 hours.

2. Preheat oven to 450 degrees. Heat the rest of the olive oil
   (1 tablespoon) on medium-high heat in an ovenproof skillet.
   Put the chicken in the pan, skin side down, with the garlic and
   herbs. Now weight the chicken with another heavy skillet, and a
   brick or a couple of heavy rocks. Cook on medium-high heat
   for 10 minutes.

150

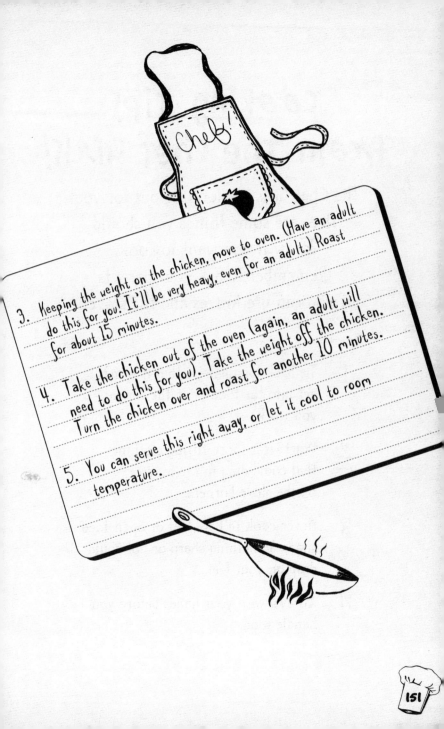

3. Keeping the weight on the chicken, move to oven. (Have an adult do this for you! It'll be very heavy, even for an adult.) Roast for about 15 minutes.

4. Take the chicken out of the oven (again, an adult will need to do this for you). Take the weight off the chicken. Turn the chicken over and roast for another 10 minutes.

5. You can serve this right away, or let it cool to room temperature.

cooking tips
from the chef Girls!

The Chef Girls are looking out for you!
Here are some things you should
know if you want to cook.
(Remember to ask your parents
if you can use knives and the stove!)

1   Tie back long hair so that it won't
    get into the food or in the way as
    you work.

2   Don't wear loose-fitting clothing
    that could drag in the food or
    on the stove burners.

3   Never cook in bare feet or open-toed
    shoes. Something sharp or hot could
    drop on your feet.

4   Always wash your hands before you
    handle food.

5   Read through the recipe before you start. Gather your ingredients together and measure them before you begin.

6   Turn pot handles in so that they won't get knocked off the stove.

7   Use wooden spoons to stir hot liquids. Metal spoons can become very hot.

8   When cutting or peeling food, cut away from your hands.

9   Cut food on a cutting board, not the countertop.

10   Hand someone a knife with the knifepoint pointing to the floor.

11   Clean up as you go. It's safer and neater.

12   Always use a dry pot holder to remove something hot from the oven. You could get burned with a wet one, since wet ones retain heat.

13   Make sure that any spills on the floor are cleaned up right away, so that you don't slip and fall.

14 Don't put knives in clean-up water. You could reach into the water and cut yourself.

15 Use a wire rack to cool hot baking dishes to avoid scorch marks on the countertop.

An Important Message from the Chef Girls!

Some foods can carry bacteria, such as salmonella, that can make you sick.
To avoid salmonella, always cook poultry, ground beef, and eggs thoroughly before eating.
Don't eat or drink foods containing raw eggs.
And wash hands, kitchen work surfaces, and utensils with soap and water immediately after they have been in contact with raw meat or poultry.

Instant messaging dictionary! diSh

Wuzzup What's up?

:-@ surprise or shock

GMTA Great Minds Think Alike

LOL Laughing Out Loud

G2G Got To Go

b-b Bye-Bye

L8R Later, as in "See ya later!"

Mwa smooching sound

<3 hearts